MOONSHINE

CHRONOLOGY, CALANDRA BOOKS

MOONSHINE

SUSAN DEXTER

WILDSIDE PRESS

This book is for
Elizabeth, Nikki, Shelly, and the rest of Mrs. Cercell's
Third Grade class at John F. Kennedy Elementary,
who shared *their* unicorn stories with me.

Published by Wildside Press LLC.
www.wildsidebooks.com

WIZARD'S BRAT

Wizards can't cross running water.

Tristan's hands clamped tight to the sides of the row-boat. Splinters stabbed him. Ignoring the pain, he held on anyway. He struggled to swallow down his fear. *This is the harbor. This water doesn't truly run—it just sloshes from one side to the other. Like a bucket. A really big bucket.*

The other two boys were laughing at him. He'd shut his eyes the second they'd pushed off from the quay, which they found hilarious. Tristan opened his eyes. No use. The sky, the diving, shrieking gulls, the moored boats—nothing he saw had reality. Tristan's attention could not stretch so far as the weathered buildings that lined Dunehollow's shabby wharves. All he was aware of was the *water*. He was surrounded by it. *Running water.* Water wide as the world. It stretched *forever*.

The oars squealed and clattered in the rowlocks. Every stroke pulled the battered dory farther out into the harbor.

Rho, the butcher's boy, elbowed Jock, whose father owned the boat. "Ever see a face that color?"

"Only on a fish!" Jock scoffed.

"I'm all right," Tristan said faintly. He held his lips stiff and ordered his eyes to stay open. A wizard needed a strong will. Rather than look at the water, he fixed his gaze on the boys' faces. Jock with his freckles as numberless as fish-scales. Rho pale, spending most days indoors, holding his master's knives to the grindstone.

"Maybe *he* should row," Jock suggested nastily. "Come over here, you," he ordered.

Tristan stared. The command made no sense to him. The dory bobbed, losing headway as Jock stopped working the oars. Ripples too small to be waves slapped its sides.

The fisherman's son rose up from his seat into a crouch, facing Tristan. Evidently he meant for them to change places. Tristan shook his head and stayed where he was. His grip on the dory's sides tightened till his fingers went white as bone.

"Come on—rowing won't kill you." The dory dipped and jigged. Jock adjusted to the motion effortlessly. "Whatcha afraid of?"

"We'll tip," Tristan answered honestly. As he spoke, a tiny wave broke over the dory's left side. The boat's bottom already had an inch of water sloshing back and forth across it. How much more would it take to sink them? Tristan had no idea, and feared every incoming drop.

Jock sat back heavily—likely being rough on purpose. The boat bucked like a horse on a cold morning. More water cascaded in. Tristan shut his eyes helplessly. His fingers struggled to grow into the boat's wooden sides—except all magic was useless over running water. Like wizards. And wizards' terrified apprentices.

"If you're sick in this boat, you'll swim home," Jock told him.

"If he can," Rho snickered. "My Gran says wizards hate water worse'n cats do."

"Oh, cats swim fine—once they're taught to!" All the harbor cats walked wide of Jock, for whenever he saw a chance, Jock "taught them to swim" by booting them off the edge of the quay. Tristan had seen him hard at his work, last time he came to Dunehollow.

And still Tristan had been tricked, just the same as the cats. Jock lured the cats with bits of food. He'd tempted the wizard's apprentice with friendship. Jock had casually invited Tristan to join him and Rho for a trip to the jetty. They'd look for gull's eggs, Jock said. Tristan knew better than to get into *any* boat, but apparently he wasn't as smart as the cats. He got into the dory anyway.

Tristan's master, Blais, sent his apprentice to Dune-hollow-by-the-Sea regularly. Tristan delivered potions to those folk who'd ordered them the week past, took orders from any who didn't need to consult with Blais in person. Gentle salves for hands crippled by damp and hard work were popular. Women wanted charms to keep fishermen safe, or lovers faithful. Tristan doled out paper-labeled dark bottles, clay jars sealed with red wax. He collected whatever payments were due in exchange—though too often of late he got only promises. His last chore before heading home would be to buy a fresh-caught fish, which he'd cook for the evening meal. Leftovers would enrich the mess of vegetable stew that simmered perpetually in the pot.

Blais had not ordered his apprentice to get himself straight home once his work was done. It wasn't necessary. At fourteen, Tristan was no child—he was a wizard in training. He was expected to know better than to waste his time idling about the village. He had no reason to linger in Dunehollow anyway. It wasn't as if he had friends there.

The *hope* of friends was the bait that coaxed Tristan into the wretched boat. He'd ignored the sly look behind Jock's open words, though he'd seen it. Tristan wasn't a fool. But he'd wanted—just this one time—for the offer to be real. He'd wanted to believe that if he wasn't being called "wizard's brat" every other breath, it might just be *possible* for him to make a friend.

He was, after all, a fool. Jock and Rho didn't want or need a friend panicked by something as commonplace in their lives as ordinary open water. They'd only wanted a victim. One more fun to torment than the wary cats. And Tristan had obliged.

The rowlocks shrieked to life. The dory swung. Jock was putting the boat about. Incredibly, he was making for the quay. Tristan put his head on his knees, relieved and bitterly ashamed of his weakness.

The dory bumped the stone quay, bobbed and bumped again as Rho scrambled out. Tristan made to follow the butcher's boy, but Jock shoved past, carrying the mooring rope. Probably he was going to tie up the boat, Tristan decided.

Instead, Jock gave the rowboat a mighty shove as he left it. The dory shot back a dozen feet. Emptied of two-thirds of its cargo, it rode light as a water bug. Tristan stared astonished at the broad reach of water suddenly separating him from the quay.

"Swim for it," Jock suggested pleasantly. Behind him, Rho leaned over and held his sides, laughing himself breathless. No question that pushing the boat off had been deliberate.

Tristan sat frozen, his hands still on the boat's sides. He tried to will the craft to stop moving. Of course, no magic worked upon or across running water, and certainly not mere wishes. He couldn't *make* the boat drift back to the quay. Tristan stared helplessly up at Jock, who still held the end of the mooring rope. That rope was the dory's only link to dry, solid land.

"*Please,*" Tristan whispered. He didn't want to scream. He didn't want to beg. He knew he might need to do both, all the same, to make Jock pull the boat back to land. His tormentors hadn't had *nearly* the fun they could expect to wring out of him. Not yet.

"Did you hear something?" Jock cupped a hand around his left ear. Rho was still doubled over. He shook his head weakly at Jock's question.

"Please," Tristan repeated, a bit louder. "Please pull the boat back." As if they didn't know what he wanted! He noticed that Jock had taken the oars with him too.

"Pull you back?" Jock pretended to be confused. "What with?" He tossed the rope toward the boat. It missed. One end was tied to the dory, but the other end sank straight into the black water. Tristan's heart sank with it.

Maybe he could paddle with his hands? Tristan dipped a finger into the dirty water, experimenting. He did not, of course, know how to swim. Wizards couldn't learn to swim. But he had seen that the oars pulled the boat through the water. Understanding things was important, to a wizard. Blais had taught him to keep his eyes open. Tristan did, mostly. The oars pulled, the boat moved. If he could use his hands like oars…

The boat moved. It swung left when he used his right hand, and right when he switched to his left. That was fine, Tristan decided. The movement was consistent. He could steer, knowing that. Jock had pulled both oars together and the boat had gone straight ahead. Tristan's arms were long, always too long for his sleeves. If he could reach water on both sides of the dory at once…maybe he could make the dory move without swinging from one side to the other.

The instant Tristan worked the boat close to the quay, Jock used an oar to shove it away again. Tristan had been expecting the trick. He doggedly coaxed the boat back. It was no use moving to another spot—wherever he went, Jock would be there waiting for him. Jock could walk along the quay, or even run. Tristan's paddling improved, but he did not think he could take the dory clear to the next village. Being out on the water made him dizzy. He was cold. He could barely feel his fingers. And the dory was still taking on water. Much of the caulking was missing from between the splintery planks, and water trickled in steadily.

If it actually *sank*, would Jock be in trouble? Tristan decided he would likely drown before he found out. He wouldn't have a chance to enjoy the justice of whatever punishment Jock's heavy-handed father dealt out.

Next time he got near enough, Tristan grabbed hold of a piling, one of the quay's wooden supports. If he dared to crawl around the thick post, maybe he could climb out onto the quay. It wouldn't be very much harder than climbing the apple tree beside the cottage, Unless he fell out of the boat, trying.

Jock used his oar to rock the boat, then jabbed Tristan hard in the ribs with the butt end. Tristan let go of the piling. He wobbled and sat down, missing the narrow seat. He landed smack in the water washing over the dory's leaky bottom, a stinking mess of fish scales and old bait Jock had left in the dory after its last use. Tristan's clothes were soaked before he could get back onto the seat. He felt fortunate, though. Probably Jock had intended him to miss the boat entirely.

"Must be lovely to be a powerful wizard," Rho said conversationally.

"And never have to work for his keep," Jock agreed. "No nets to mend. No fish to gut."

"Just waggle his fingers and have whatever he wants."

"Why don't he try that now?" Jock wondered. "Suppose he don't *know* what he wants? I thought wizards was clever."

"Please," Tristan begged. "Let me get out."

Jock and Rho exchanged glances. Jock shrugged. "All you needed to do was ask," he said cheerfully, as if a mystery had been cleared up.

Jock flopped a rope ladder out over the edge of the quay. The tide was going out, and the harbor water was dropping. Rho had only needed to scramble, but now climbing straight from the boat to the quay would be difficult.

Tristan stared at the dangling ladder. The rope was black with age and dripping wet. It looked as inviting as a garden slug, all softness and slime. Tristan adored it. To his eyes, it was as precious as if it had been woven of spun gold. He splashed the rowboat closer, reached out, and caught hold of one of the ladder's sides. Shaking, he raised himself to a crouch. He put one foot on the side of the boat and tightened his grip on the ladder. Leaning forward, he stepped for the lowest of the rope rungs.

As his weight came onto it, the ladder whipped down the side of the quay. Too late, Tristan realized that it wasn't fastened to anything at all! Jock wasn't even still holding it. Tristan flailed, struggling desperately to fall into the boat. He knew he wouldn't make it. The dory tipped hard under him, then turned turtle.

As he went headlong into the water, Tristan heard shouts of laughter from the quay above. Then the water clogged his ears, and he heard nothing more except his own heart, pounding in terror.

* * * *

He surely went, Tristan thought, clear to the bottom of the harbor. Though it was dark down there, and he could see no clear details. The light above him looked as far away as the moon, impossibly distant. He kicked frantically toward it. To his amazement, he shot flailing to the surface.

That did him no good. Tristan struck out with both hands in a panic, but touched only air, then water. He promptly went under a second time. Not so deeply as his first plunge—but the one gasp he'd barely had time for had been as much salt water as air. The smelly harbor water burned up his nose and did nothing to ease his lungs. Tristan kicked for the surface again.

His clothes were full of water and weighed like lead. He seemed to have no strength in his legs. Tristan struggled with all his might, but only his left hand broke the surface before he began to go down again.

Something poked him hard in the middle of his back. Tristan felt a flicker of anger. Jock was using the oar to push him back under! What was the point, when he was already drowning? Wasn't he being quick enough about it?

All at once, he was yanked upward. Tristan sailed through welcome air, then was deposited face down on the quay. The stones bruised his knees, his elbows, his chin— but at least he couldn't sink through them. Tristan sprawled, gasping, spitting up water.

The old sail-mender disengaged the boathook from Tristan's belt. He dropped the tool onto the quay next to the boy. "Catch the oddest fish in these waters," he chuck-led. "Some of 'em worth keepin'." His own wit seemed to amuse him. "You all right, boy?" He poked Tristan's shoul-der with one callused finger.

Tristan was too busy trying to cough his lungs inside out to answer. When he *could* speak, he tried to thank the old man. No one else was around, Tristan noticed. No sign of Jock, or Rho. He overlooked the two shining green eyes watching the show from the shadow of an overturned lob-ster trap.

The old fisherman brushed his thanks away. "Eh, those rascals! They run like harbor rats when I come along. You go on home, boy. Stay away from the likes of they. Stupid, they are, and mean too."

Tristan was only too happy to do as he was told. His clothes were heavy with water, and clung so that he could scarcely drag one foot after the other. His boots were still on his feet, an unexpected mercy. They sloshed nastily as he walked straight out of Dunehollow-by-the-Sea as fast as he could stagger. Not till he was well on the road home did Tristan finally pause to squeeze some of the water from his clothing.

Suddenly he remembered the fish. The fish for supper. The fish he was supposed to buy. Tristan hastily thrust his hand into his deepest pocket, seeking the copper coin for the fishmonger.

The pocket was empty. So were all its mates. Tristan checked every one, though he knew perfectly well where he'd tucked the solitary coin.

The copper had gone to the bottom of Dunehollow's harbor. Tristan heartily wished he'd done the same.

CAT ON HIS OWN

Three minutes after he'd passed the last house on the raggedy outer edge of Dunehollow, Tristan sat down beside a bramble bush. His heavy boots had squeaked and squelched with his every step. When he sat, they sulkily fell silent.

Tristan's feet felt awful. His toes were cold, but not too chilled to notice that they were drowning. His thick socks had soaked up all the seawater they could, then surrendered. Their rough wool sawed with every step he took, back and forth. Either the socks were coming to pieces, or his skin was blistering. Maybe both. The one would help the other.

Tristan tugged off his left boot and dumped harbor water out of it. He left the boot upended while he dragged its mate from his right foot. More water. No copper coin. He had not really thought it might be there. And there wasn't room in his boots for even a *small* fish to be trapped. Not that he'd expected to find one of those, either.

The wind blew, cold even with the brambles breaking its force. Tristan sighed. He watched water dripping from his sleeve onto his sock. Ought to check his pockets for fish as well, he thought. He might find the makings for a chowder.

He needed to get himself dry, before he went homeward. He was chilled to the bone just from the soaking. If he let the wind dry his clothes as he walked, he could certainly expect to pay for the service—the fee would be aching bones, fever, and a cruelly stuffed nose. Not to mention sneezing and coughing. All his master's herb-lore would not prevent his catching cold, though Tristan knew he would not die of the complaint. He'd only *wish* he might.

With a wizard's firestone, he could kindle a fire and dry his clothes. Warm his feet. Tristan had often used his master's firestone, but he didn't yet have one of his own. One of an apprentice's tasks was to find or make his own magical tools. Tristan had searched, but he hadn't found a firestone yet.

So if he wanted a blaze, he must rub two sticks together till they caught fire. Tristan shivered. He'd never, ever, been able to start a fire that way. Nor could he strike flint and steel together to make a spark—iron was deadly poison to anyone who dealt in magic, and he never had any of the metal on him.

The wind felt colder every moment. Maybe he should go back to the village. He could beg a coal at one of the houses. Maybe the baker wouldn't ask questions.

Tristan decided he would rather dare the stopped-up nose and sneezing fits. Another idea teased him till he considered it. If he could wring the worst of the water from his clothes, they'd be a lot drier than they were. Drier should be warmer. There was a spell he used when he washed the linens in the stream beside his master's cottage...he could try that! The principle of it was exactly the same.

Tristan positioned his fingers with care. He stretched one out straight, cocked another back till his wrist ached. He spoke a strangely accented, precise string of words and moved his last finger in a tiny circle in time to his lips. Squinting with concentration, Tristan turned his right hand sunwards and his left hand widdershins. Exactly as if he were wringing out wet laundry...

Instantly, water began dripping out of the young wizard's clothes. Water streamed from the ragged hems of his trews, ran out of his sleeve ends. Water dripped through his hair and rolled down his nose. Water squirted out of his socks. A puddle formed on the ground about his feet.

Tristan could not hold back a surprised laugh. He hadn't expected the spell to work. His magic so seldom did what he wished it to—but there it was! Every last thread of his clothing was busily twisting the water out of itself. Soon he'd be dry as toasted bread.

His skin itched as the threads writhed and crawled over it. Tristan ignored the unpleasant sensation. The spell had nearly run its course. The wringing would stop soon enough, and he'd pull his boots on, go home, and face his master in dry clothes.

Suddenly Tristan heard—and *felt*—threads popping. Fibers snapped from the strain of constant twisting. They broke by ones and twos, then by the dozen. Patches sewn over the worn spots on his trews flew off like square birds. Threadbare spots became actual holes, then long rents. Seams opened like plowed furrows, unraveling while Tristan stared helplessly.

The knitted wool of his pullover tightened up, as if the garment was being boiled. The twisted yarns hugged one another tightly. They never let go. Tristan's sleeve-ends—which had not reached his wrist-bones since his growth spurt the spring past—wormed toward his elbows. The ribbed collar choked him. Tristan got two fingers inside it only just in time. He pulled against the knitting for all he was worth. He tugged, he yanked, and at last something tore. Tristan gasped out a breathless counter-spell, but by the time the garbled dismissal took effect, the damage was done.

Tristan sighed, trying not to let his breath out as an actual sob.

At least his clothes were dry, he told himself. Wrecked, they were, but *dry*.

That was how his magic worked! Quirky, backward, random. Perverse in every way it possibly could be. Uncontrollable, no matter how much care he took with it. Blais had often assured his apprentice that the persons who'd abandoned an infant son in his orchard would only have done so for the most desperate of reasons. Lately, Tristan suspected those strangers had somehow known *exactly* the sort of child they were ridding themselves of, that midwinter night fourteen years back.

A twig snapped, very near.

Tristan jerked his head up. Jock? Rho? Sneaking up with more pranks in mind? It was a moment before he noticed a little cat standing at the edge of the road, staring at him with narrowed green eyes.

You smell like fish, the cat said. Its mouth was open slightly, but its whiskered lips did not move to shape the words. Tristan heard a dry voice in his head, very clearly.

"I fell in the harbor," he explained, aloud. He didn't assume the creature could read his thoughts, though maybe it could. "That water always stinks of fish-guts."

The cat was a well-grown kitten. Old enough to roam free of its mother, but only just. Its rabbit-color fur was tabby marked with stripes and spots of black, and it looked as if it might grow longer as the kitten grew older. Tail well up, it strolled toward Tristan.

The green eyes narrowed further. *So you don't actually have any fish?*

"No." Tristan held out his hand politely. Except for reaching, he kept it still. It was unmannerly to grab at cats. Cats scratched when you were rude.

The cat butted its round head against his fingers. *Pity. Fish is very nice.*

"Harbor cats have trouble getting fish?" Whenever a boat came in, the cats of Dunehollow swarmed the quay. The gulls did likewise. The two sorts of creatures mewed and screamed at one another, setting up a racket until they were given—or had stolen—their fill of fish.

I am not meant to be a harbor cat. I have a destiny. My mother told me so. The cat sniffed delicately at a thread dangling from Tristan's sleeve. *I am Thomas.*

"Pleased to meet you. I'm Tristan." At least, that was the name Blais had given his foundling. If Tristan had more of a name than that, he wasn't likely ever to know it. He sighed again, feeling sorry for himself. Not, he decided, without proper cause.

Are you going to sit here all day? The cat curled his tail around his paws and regarded Tristan with unblinking curiosity.

Tristan wished he *could* just stay where he was, possibly for the entire rest of his life. He didn't relish explaining to his master about the fish he hadn't bought. He didn't want to confess losing the only cash money they'd earned in a month. *Could* he just sit till hunger and thirst made an end to him and his misery?

Probably not. People would pass by on the road and object to his loitering beside it. Jock might discover him. Blas might even search him out. Tristan pulled his boots on, with some difficulty. The wet leather needed oiling. It was going to stiffen. The left boot was starting to lose its sole. The heel was coming off the right. Tristan used a small rock to hammer the pegs back in, which would hold the boots together for a few miles more.

He lurched to his feet. No use tugging at his sleeve ends. His pullover was a good deal smaller than it had been when he'd pulled it on that morning. Loose threads hung from it like grass from a robin's nest. Tristan decided he had best not pull at any of them. He'd be walking home naked as a newly hatched bird, if the knitting unraveled.

After a hundred paces, he noticed the cat was following him.

"I don't have any fish," Tristan reminded him. "I was supposed to fetch some, but I lost the money."

What about a cow? I like cream, the dry voice informed him, rather hopefully.

"So do I! It's the only thing that makes pease porridge worthwhile." Tristan frowned. "We have a milk cow, and we have chickens, and we have kept a pig, from time to time. And a beehive, for honey and candle-wax."

No cat?

"My master's never said anything about wanting a cat," Tristan told him, hoping the cat would catch the hint.

Then the position's open. Evidently his hint had gone unnoticed.

"I don't know," Tristan said uneasily. "I really think you'd better be going back."

The cat ignored his advice. In fact, it strode past Tristan, tail hoisted high, and walked on as if it knew its way perfectly well. After a moment, Tristan hurried after it.

"It's a long walk," he tried again.

Any dogs at your place? The tail was still high, but the cat's tufted ears tipped back, just a bit.

"Dogs? No, no dogs. But—"

Good. The ears came back up to a jaunty angle. *Not that dogs are a problem, you understand. My mother taught me all about dealing with dogs. No worries there.*

"But I can't...I can't just bring you home with me," Tristan explained. "It's bad enough I'll be back without the fish for supper."

Oh, fish. Eat it once, it's gone for good. Whereas a good cat...did I mention that I catch mice?

"I bet you catch birds, too," Tristan said.

Certainly. I am a skilled hunter. That sounded like a bluff. Thomas was surely too young to have gathered much experience.

Tristan pounced anyway. "Well, that's no good! My master *loves* birds! Blais won't let you stay."

Thomas brushed the objection away. *I might agree not to chase anything feathered. In exchange, say, for the occasional saucer of fresh cream.* The cat stopped and looked up at Tristan. Its little pink mouth was open slightly, panting. *This is rather a far piece of walking,* it said. *With your long legs, you probably don't notice it...*

Tristan sighed. He bent down. Thomas allowed himself to be picked up. The small cat snuggled against what was left of the tortured pullover, purring loudly enough for a creature three times his size.

AN INEPT APPRENTICE

"No," Blais said firmly.

"But he'll catch mice!" Tristan persisted.

"And what else?" Blais arched one brow high. "Mice do not trouble me, Tristan. A few simple wards keep them out of the larder and the barn. The field mice and the voles in the meadow harm no one. And I do not wish to be finding dead birds on my doorstep."

Tristan felt his carefully thought-out arguments for the usefulness of a cat dissolving like mist in the sun. He should have remembered that he'd never seen a mouse inside the cottage—and understood *why*. A wizard who could set magical barriers that kept rodents from crossing his threshold scarcely needed a cat to do the same work. And Blais plainly didn't *want* a cat.

"Thomas wouldn't hunt birds," Tristan began again, but the ploy lacked force, and Blais pushed it aside.

"It is a cat's nature to hunt. They cannot help it. No creature can be other than it is, Tristan."

"He won't hunt birds if I ask him not to!"

Blais frowned at his apprentice's refusal to let be. The lack of resemblance between the two could not have been greater. Tristan was two fingers taller than his master already and plainly nowhere near done with his over-hasty growing. Blais' hair and beard both curled, and had once been the color of clean sand. The stress of raising an abandoned infant and struggling to turn him into a wizard had turned every last hair white. It was the only transformation that had been completely successful. Tristan was still a long way from becoming a wizard. A distressingly long way, some days.

The apprentice's chin was bare, so far, but the thick hair on Tristan's head was dark as a sparrow's wing and grew straight as spider silk. Tristan pushed it back out of his eyes so often that he continued to do so even now, when it was sheared even with his brows and could not possibly blind him. His green eyes held an anxious look—but not a trace of hope.

Tristan had, Blais saw, made an effort to mend his spell-wrecked clothes. Fresh patches shone bright on both knees, as well as across his seat. Each repair was firmly stitched with strong thread. Tristan could not yet trust *magical* mending to hold—more was the pity. Because he got more practice at it, the boy's darning was better than his spell-casting by far. Tristan seemed to grow out of his clothes while he slept, and when awake he found countless ways to rip, tear or burn holes in the cloth. The kitten's claws had added a few new snags.

Blais sighed. It wasn't Tristan's fault. The cast-off clothes were barely worth mending. The boy never complained, and he tried his best to learn his lessons. At infrequent intervals, he showed real promise in magic. At other times...times like this...there were too many times like this, Blais thought. It was enough to make a wizard despair.

He kept his emotions hidden. It would be cruel to let Tristan see his concern. Kinder to be stern with the boy. Pity could sting more sharply than any blow.

The boy was lonely. His ventures to Dunehollow had netted him trouble a-plenty, but had yet to produce a friend. Tristan had never seemed to want a pet, but Blais decided the idea was not entirely without merit. Perhaps a rabbit—no, then there'd be no more meat for the stew-pot.

Too much like eating family. Perhaps a squirrel. One of the little flying ones. Soft, gentle creatures, attractive and harmless. Squirrels didn't kill for sport and weren't worth eating either.

"I don't forbid pets," the wizard said gently, his thoughts come full circle. "But a cat can never help being a cat. You must not expect this one to change his nature simply because you wish it, Tristan."

Tristan's forehead was furrowed ever so slightly. What else *was* magic, but bending creatures and forces to a wizard's will? He said nothing. His curiosity might sound insolent, put into words. Tristan knew he had learned no magic that would keep Thomas from hunting birds, if he could not trust the cat's word. Trust was his failing—he had trusted Jock and Rho, after all. Maybe he shouldn't want to trust a strange cat.

"You can take him back to Dunehollow—where he no doubt has family missing him—tomorrow. I shall be off myself at first light. I have been called to consult with Master Sedwick," Blais told him. "I should be back within the week. You will look after things here, as usual. There's plenty of meal for porridge and cakes. No one has ordered any charms except the usual for the cabbage moths. I shall attend to that when I return."

"*I* could—" Tristan began hopefully, raising his head.

"Best if you wait till I'm back," Blais said, squelching the hope at once. He rested a hand on Tristan's shoulder and squeezed to command his apprentice's attention. "The moths may not be the whole trouble with those cabbages. The spell may need to be recast, before 'twill be effective. You will learn how to do so by watching me, not by muddling through on your own. If a wizard appears uncertain, his clients may refuse him his payment." Blais sighed. "For now, go and start supper."

"Porridge?" Tristan asked in a very small voice. Blais had also sighed over the matter of the fish. That resigned sound had hurt worse than any beating Rho ever got from *his* master.

"Or oatcakes," his master suggested. "You might ask the bees for a comb of honey."

Tristan nodded, a little cheered. He could never get enough of sweets, and usually the honey their bees made went into Blais' potions. Tristan started toward the cottage, thinking happily about the honey. He noticed Thomas prowling along the little stream, stalking through the waving grass on the bank.

Tristan tried convincing himself that he didn't *need* a pet. Especially a pet apt to make him presents of small dead animals. He hadn't considered that. Tristan had nothing against sparrows and moles—he rather liked the little creatures.

His efforts failed miserably. He remembered the way Thomas had sought him out, had chosen to stay with him. Been his friend. The pit of his stomach felt empty. It wasn't hunger—though he *was* hungry, Tristan decided. Too bad they wouldn't be having fish for their supper. Fried up in a pan or added to a chowder, either choice was good and filling.

He always seemed to be hungry. From growing, Blais said. Tristan sometimes wondered if he would be done with growing while he could still get through the cottage's doorway without ducking.

A splash interrupted wistful thoughts of dinners that might have been. Tristan glanced toward the stream. He didn't see a cat on the bank. He heard another splash and then a choked squall.

Supper forgotten, Tristan sprinted toward the water.

He spied Thomas at once, splashing furiously in a pool. Something thrashed beneath the cat. Tristan saw the flick of a tail-fin, a flash of dappled scales. *A trout!* Evidently, Thomas' plunge had not been accidental.

The fish was nearly the young cat's match for weight and too much for him to master in deep water. Thomas wrapped his paws around the trout. He yowled and sputtered as the fish took him under. Tristan teetered for a heartbeat on the bank, then leaped in after him.

Blais, drawn by the commotion, raised his hands—but a wizard could cast no magic over or into running water. Tristan's master strode down the bank instead, watching anxiously. The stream was deep enough to drown a cat, but not an apprentice unless the apprentice worked at it. Slippery rocks frustrated Tristan's efforts to get to his feet, but mostly his head stayed above the surface. Even in running water, he wasn't in any real danger.

Finally, the current pushed him against a snag of drifted wood. Tristan tried to climb out, using the hand that wasn't holding the cat to seize a twisted branch. He slipped, went under, came up sputtering—still with the cat clutched to his chest. Tristan groped blindly for the drifted tree. Blais reached past his fingers, caught hold of Tristan's sleeve, and heaved. With a ripping sound, boy, cat—and trout— flopped out onto the muddy bank.

Tristan coughed helplessly, sprawled on the wet ground. To be nearly drowned *twice* in the same day! It was completely unfair! Thomas wriggled out from under him. The cat gave the trout a hard bite on the back of its head, and the fish ceased its thrashing. Thomas shook water from his fur, mostly onto Tristan.

Fish, he announced unnecessarily.

* * * *

"That's a fox track," Blais pointed to the ground beside the hen coop. "This one is bold. He's been testing the wards every night. You must watch out for him, Tristan. Don't neglect the wards, or forget to re-set them at sunfall."

Tristan nodded. The protective wards were dismissed during the day, so the hens could forage for bugs in the yard. They caught most of their own food, that way.

"I could sleep out here," he offered. "Give the fox a surprise if he gets in."

His master's mouth twisted. "Just set the wards. A grown fox would make a worse pet than a cat."

Tristan began to protest, but Blais shushed him and took the sack of oatcakes his apprentice had baked for his journey-food. "Don't forget to milk the cow morning *and* evening. And see if you can't churn some butter. Sedwick will likely send some of his new potatoes home with me."

* * * *

"You still have to go, Thomas. Blais was very firm about that." Tristan scrubbed fiercely at the porridge pot. He'd been careless of the fire. Besides burnt porridge for breakfast, he had the work of cleaning the scorched pot.

Didn't he like the fish? Thomas asked. The cat tossed a tiny pebble from paw to paw. The pebble escaped, and he sprang at the shadow it cast as it rolled across the sunlit floor.

"Well, it was more fish than *I'd* managed to fetch for him." Tristan scowled glumly at the pot. Scorched oatmeal was stubborn. Next time the cottage walls needed patching, he'd know just what to use. "*I* liked it. I can never catch a trout. Not even with a silver hook. But Blais still says I have to take you back to Dunehollow. He reminded me just before he left. You were sitting right there. You must have heard him."

As if you could make me stay there. Thomas batted the stone again, then captured the pebble. He held it to his mouth as if to bite it.

"I can't let you stay *here*," Tristan said. "As soon as I've cleaned this—" the last of the oatmeal finally gave up the fight. The copper pot shone pink. "And swept out the hearth, we'd better go." He wiped the pot dry and picked up the twig broom.

Why do wizards fuss with brooms and dish-rags? What good's magic? Thomas hooked the tips of his claws into the broom. He tussled with it until Tristan pulled it out of his reach.

"Blais doesn't need magic for housekeeping. He has *me*. That's what apprentices are for. And *I* don't use magic to sweep the floor because—" Tristan fell silent, not sure how much the cat understood. Had Thomas seen the clothes-drying fiasco? And would he assume the affliction applied to other chores?

I *could*, though, Tristan thought stubbornly. He chewed at his bottom lip. Do thus, and so. And then so again. He could remove every last trace of ash from the hearth in the space of two breaths. *Much* faster than scraping ashes and cinders into a pile, scooping the pile into the scuttle, and lugging the heavy scuttle all the way to the midden. Ashes scattered out on every wisp of breeze, and he always had to sweep the floor again after.

Blais had used a spell the week past, removing a rotten egg from a pancake batter. He'd even made the stink of the bad egg vanish from the air. Tristan examined the spell in his memory. It was important for wizards to observe and remember what they saw. Yes, *that*. And the fingerplay just *so*, to dismiss the unwanted object. He did know the spell. Every word, every gesture. He understood its principles. He could use it.

Tristan put the broom down. He set the scuttle aside. Squaring his shoulders, he faced the hearth. Thomas pricked his ears with interest.

Tristan raised his right hand. He held it up with the first finger pointed, while he made gathering gestures with his left hand. His lips twisted around insistent words. Ashes clumped obediently. Tristan lowered his right hand, aiming his forefinger at the hearth. Instead of a word, a puff of plain air left his lips.

Whoooosh! The ashes started up the chimney, vanishing even as they rose. Tristan's ears popped. He blinked.

Thomas crouched by his feet. The cat's fur stood on end. His eyes squinched nearly shut. *Well, welllll*, the cat purred, obviously impressed.

* * * *

"I don't why Blais didn't want me to tend to the cabbage moths," Tristan grumbled as they neared the outskirts of Dunehollow-by-the-Sea. "All I'd need to do is call up some dragonflies and get them to notice the moths. They'd do the rest. It's hardly even a *spell*."

Thomas, draped over his left shoulder like a coat, boxed Tristan lightly on the ear. *You're as witless obedient as a dog,* the cat hissed. *You're wasting your time hauling me back here. I won't stay. I intend to see the world and find my fortune. Not to mention my destiny.*

"Just don't start off by following me home again," Tristan advised him. "If he wants to, bad eggs aren't the only things Blais can make disappear."

Thomas purred very loudly, his whole body vibrating against Tristan's shoulder and neck. *He won't hurt me. And he won't order me to go—or to come when he calls.*

"Well, fine for you! But *I'm* Blais' apprentice, and *I* have to do what Blais says!" He stopped suddenly, attention caught. *"What's that?"*

Tristan had no intention of going anywhere *near* the harbor, so he'd turned into the first alley he came to. The narrow passage linked a few back gardens with one of the lesser streets. The shouts and shriekings suddenly filling the air would have suited the butcher's slaughtering pen, only Tristan knew Rho's master kept shop at the far end of the village. And the shrieks were human words, not swine squeals.

"Help! Murder!"

"Fire! Ho! Fetch water!"

One hand steadying Thomas, Tristan hurried onward. He reached a larger street and turned along it in the direction of the Guildhall. That was an easy landmark—no other structure in Dunehollow boasted a full three storeys. The shouts were much louder. People rushed toward the hall from all directions. From streets and shops they came, out of houses and up from the harbor.

"Help! The Mayor! The Mayor's murdered!"

"Thought 'twas a fire!" shouted a man with a pail.

Instinct halted Tristan where he was. Instead of running straight out into the square, he ducked into another narrow street. He ran down an alley, dodged a jumble of lobster traps, and finally stretched to peer over a wobbly fence.

He saw a score of folk milling in front of the Guildhall's shallow steps. More people joined them with buckets in hand. They jostled one another and called questions. At the foot of the stair stood a man. The crowd had left a little space around him, so Tristan could see him clearly.

The Mayor's girth was impressive. The man could afford to eat well. His shape was exactly like the wine barrels which supplied his living at the tavern he owned. Newly come from conducting official business in the hall, the Mayor was dressed in his best. He wore fine britches and polished shoes, a pale starched shirt and what must have been a fine waistcoat.

Very little of his grand costume was actually visible. From head to toe, the Mayor of Dunehollow was coated with fine gray ash. Cinders were heaped about his feet.

"Come out of the air, it did!" a woman cried. "The sky clear as could be, not so much as a gull flying over. And then all this—"

The Mayor coughed. The Mayor sneezed. The Mayor's eyes, when he opened them, were red as blood and full of fury. His Honor tried to issue an order to his bailiffs, but another fit of coughing afflicted him. Clouds of ash puffed off of him with his every movement.

"Oh, *no!*" Tristan moaned, behind the fence. He had that horrible emptiness in the pit of his stomach again. He recognized those ashes. He could smell, very clearly, the apple-wood scent of the cottage's hearth-fire. "Oh, *noooo!*"

A DARK MOON

Light a candle, Thomas suggested. The cat flicked his tail impatiently.

Tristan shook his head. "I don't think so!" Suppose someone saw that light? It would draw them straight to the cottage. Blais' home sat at the end of an obvious path, beside the orchard's carefully-tended trees. There was nothing to hide the place. Not even—yet—darkness. Though the cottage was dim inside, the sky was still light.

Tristan had shoved the heavy work table against the cottage door, in too much haste to bother with the incantation that would have compelled the table to walk over on its own legs. A thick oak plank further barred the door. Tristan had added a lock-ward for good measure. Now he sat under the table, his back pressed against the door. His eyes were shut tight. He held his breath much of the time.

Thomas finished sharpening his claws upon the windowsill and jumped to the floor. He marched over to Tristan and peered up at him. He sniffed. *No one followed us. I told you that.*

"They didn't have to *follow* us," Tristan whispered, opening his eyes. He gave the window a wary glance, but from where he sat, he couldn't see it—the table blocked his view. "Everyone in Dunehollow knows where the wizard lives…"

So? Thomas' eyes shone, giving back the light that found its way past the closed shutters. *You think they suspect you?*

"How could they not?" Tristan asked indignantly, forgetting to whisper. "Ashes out of thin air—"

"You've done it before, then?" Thomas cocked his head, as if impressed by the notion.

"No!"

Thomas sat, wrapping his tail neatly about his paws. *Ashes are just ashes, you know,* he said conversationally.

Tristan stared at the cat. "What's *that* supposed to mean?"

You weren't there when it happened. Thomas' eyes were unblinking. *So far as they know. No one saw us in the village.*

"You think they didn't know a rain of ashes was magic?" Tristan asked scornfully.

Thomas gave one paw a delicate lick. *Fools, they surely are. Didn't they think the mayor was murdered, even when he was standing there alive, in plain sight? I didn't hear any mention of magic.* He cocked his head again. *Did you?*

Tristan leaned his head back against the door. He wondered if he'd be able to feel approaching footsteps. Hoofbeats, certainly. The earth conducted those well. Only no one in the village had a horse. Just a couple of shaggy donkeys and a pony, used to drag the fish carts around. The villagers would walk. The question was, would they keep silent? Or would they come shouting and grumbling and threatening? Would he have any sort of warning at all?

Mind, I'm not saying it wouldn't be wise to lie low, just for a bit. Thomas carefully inspected the claws of his left front paw. *Discretion always has value.*

"I'm never going back to Dunehollow again!" Tristan burst out. He meant every word of his vow. The notion that no one in the village would think him capable of even such a wretched piece of spellcraft burned like seawater on scraped skin. He should have been relieved to escape the disaster. Instead, Tristan felt so ashamed that just breathing hurt.

He scrambled to his feet. Thomas was right. No one was coming after him. He wasn't worth the bother—

Misjudging the table's edge, Tristan slammed his left shoulder hard into it. The table barely moved. Tristan sat down again, without intending to. He bit back rash words. A curse spoken now might just stick! Blais wouldn't want his table charred to a crisp.

Humans don't see well in the dark, Thomas observed in mock surprise.

Tristan got to his feet more carefully. He pickled up a candle from the tabletop. The collision had jarred it from its candlestick and cracked it right across. It leaned tipsily in Tristan's hand, held together by its wick.

Normally he'd light a candle from the cookfire. Nothing to it. However, the hearth was cold and painfully clean. Wincing, Tristan turned away. He felt across the mantel. Blais always left his firestone there, handy.

Of course Blais had taken his firestone. The walk to Master Sedwick's was longish, and Blais would pause along the way. The wizard would rest, eat a bite of food, brew himself a cup of peppermint tea. Blais could not have expected that Tristan would thoughtlessly put out the cottage fire the moment he and his firestone were gone.

Tristan sighed. He could grope about in the dark and eat a cold supper. A *raw* supper. Or he could beg a coal from the nearest neighbor, the best part of a league away. He should have had another choice. Fire-lighting was the very first spell Blais had taught him. In some ways, its magic was the basis of all the rest. To control fire, to create it, was a vital skill.

But without a firestone's aid, Tristan was helpless to summon the magic. His spell wouldn't go awry. It simply wouldn't go *anywhere*.

Thomas washed himself in earnest. The cat licked his paws one by one. He cleaned between each toe. He licked his back. He scrubbed behind his ears with a damp paw. He finished with his tail, combing and fluffing the hair. Finally he seemed satisfied. *I expect you're too upset to eat?* he asked brightly.

"I'm not hungry." Tristan decided not to mention the lack of fire. "The cow's got to be milked, though." He picked up the wooden pail.

Thomas licked his lips and headed for the door, his tail raised high as if he flew an invisible banner from it.

The sky was still bright enough to let Tristan see what he was doing. He gave the cow her evening measure of grain and settled down to milk her while she was busy with eating it. "Sit over there," he directed Thomas, pointing to a nearby spot.

After that, most of the milk was for the pail, but Tristan sent every fourth or fifth squirt Thomas' way. He was rather good at milking. Spellcraft made his fingers nimble. His touch was gentle. The cow liked that and was cooperative. The cow liked *him*.

Thomas swallowed and licked white pearls of milk from his whiskers. He looked more pleased by the moment. Tristan rested his head against the cow's warm flank. She smelled of hay. He could feel, faintly, the grinding of her teeth as she ate her grain. How much better it must be to be a cow and not an apprentice wizard.

By the time Tristan was done milking, the sky was a deep violet. A fat moon was rising behind the orchard. He need not, Tristan thought, bother about a candle after all. He opened the window shutters and left the door standing wide. The evening air was mild. The silver moonlight was easily bright enough to read by. Encouraged, he turned toward Blais' books.

They faced him from all directions. There were books absolutely everywhere. Blais bought books, traded for books, borrowed books, wrote and bound many volumes himself.

Books leaned against one another all the way across the mantelpiece. They sat amid the potted herbs on the sills of the windows. Stacks of the seldom-read held up a board which bore a bound collection of Blais' daily weather observations. Two fat books made the candlestick considerably taller. A slim book kept Blais' favorite chair sitting steady.

A precarious pile teetered on a footstool. There were books under the bed and surely books *in* the bed as well, lost in the linens. The table held its own weight again in books and thus had made such an effective barricade for the door.

Tristan looked about, touching this book, then that one. He had by no means read them all, but he had read many. Finally he found what he sought. He shuffled the stack from the three-legged stool to the floor beneath the table and carried the stool to the doorway. The moonlight poured in, solid as white paint.

His master hadn't reminded him to tend to his studies. Blais hadn't needed to. Tristan enjoyed study. If he'd had only starlight to do it by, he'd have tried his best to read. Sore eyes were not too harsh a price for knowledge. Yet, the silver moonlight was more than a replacement for the candle he could not light.

The books Tristan had chosen shared a special quality. Their pages could be read only by the moon's light. Beneath the sun, their leaves were covered with gibberish—Tristan had checked once, not quite sure Blais wasn't teasing him on the subject.

Now, the carefully written words made sentences, and sense. Tristan settled contentedly to his studies. He might not be able to work magic with his master's ease, but he never tired of *learning* about it. Reading spells and committing theories to memory were better than meat and drink. At least better than pease porridge and water.

Here, for example. Six different ways of making fog. Who'd have expected half so many? Why did *one* not suffice? It wasn't like clearing ashes away.

Tristan read, but after a few moments his attention drifted. His concentration faltered. The words on the page seemed to lose their meanings. A handful of them dimmed and disappeared altogether. Tristan blinked at the blurry page, rubbed his eyes—then shifted his suspicions to the sky. Clouds often interfered with moonlight reading. Clear night skies were the rule only during the coldest part of the winter—and then he had the distraction of frozen toes and fingers to contend with.

Tristan scanned the sky. Nary a cloud. The arch of black overhead was thoroughly spattered with stars, all sharply visible. Tristan frowned. The moon looked dull. Her usually silver face was the color of an old copper coin. Did a cloud of dust veil her? Sand, windswept from some far-distant desert, smelling of cinnamon, of costly myrrh?

All at once, Tristan's heart began to hammer. His breath came fast, but not quite fast enough. The lower edge of the moon was round no longer. A sliver of it had been pared away, as if some invisible creature gnawed upon the rind of the moon. And Tristan knew what that had to mean.

An eclipse.

Not so rare or unsettling as the darkening of the sun, but uncommon enough. Tristan stood, shedding books and

Thomas, who'd crept onto his lap. The cat protested the assault on his comfort. The books merely fluttered their pages as Tristan gathered them up again and dumped them onto the table.

An eclipse presented opportunities far greater than the chance to read his master's moonlight books. This was a special night. The moon ruled the sea. She made the tides strong or weak, high or even flooding. Spent waves cast objects up on beaches. Fantastically twisted driftwood and water-smoothed crystals appeared on the shore. Beach-gleanings provided most of the ingredients for the weather spells Blais practiced. On rough coasts, wreckers made good livings collecting what the sea spat up—lumber, wine casks, crates full of lost treasures. On a smaller scale, Tristan and his master got their livings the same way.

Wreckers greeted storms with glee. Wizards felt the same way about eclipses. Tides governed by a dark moon brought up strange things. Uncommon things. Powerful things. Wonders beyond imagining. Tristan must seek them, gather them. Such opportunities came infrequently. He could not ignore this one. He would not.

His master had told him to stay home, except for taking the cat back to Dunehollow. But Blais had not expected the eclipse. Predicting eclipses required patient observation for years on end. Records had to be kept. Charts had to be drawn. And after all the preparation, clouds might hide the moon on the critical night. In Calandra, the effort wasn't worth the chance of reward. Blais always said he preferred to take what came.

Well, now this eclipse *had* come. The wizard would not wish his apprentice to ignore it, Tristan told himself. His logic was ironclad. He looked down at Thomas.

Thomas gave an enquiring mew.

"Come on," Tristan told him.

Readying himself was no bother. Tristan slung his cloak around his shoulders and snatched up a sack to hold whatever objects he might find. His pockets were always full of holes—and who knew what wonderful things he might come across? Perhaps more than even mended pockets could safely hold.

What else? Tristan paused in the doorway, frowning. Excitement must not distract him from his responsibilities. There was something he still had to do. Something he'd forgotten. What else had Blais said?

The chickens! Tristan pulled the cottage door shut and flung a lock-spell at the weathered panel. The spell should hold, but no matter if it did not. There was nothing much inside to steal. Just the books. Few folk in Dunehollow could read, so those were safe. Tristan hurried toward the chicken coop.

The hens had all gone to roost. They were pale puffs of feathers in the gloom of the chicken house. Tristan closed the door and walked in a slow circle around the coop, weaving wards of protection as he went. His lips moved constantly, and his fingers did the same, spinning the spell till it completely enclosed the coop. *There!* Now let the fox come! The sneak-thief would find no profit in *this* night's skulking.

BEACHCOMBING

Tristan stood among grass-fringed dunes and listened to the sea. He could see, in a general sort of way. The sand was white, and there were still the stars. All the same, he missed the moon's light.

His feet knew the coast path well. He'd had small need of his eyes thus far. But here at the end, wind and waves reshaped the land on a daily basis. Tristan let his ears guide him over the last bit. Better to go around the higher dunes than to climb the wrong one and be buried in a sudden landslip of sand coming down its far side.

In the few minutes it had taken Tristan to secure the cottage and walk to the coast, the moon had fully entered the eclipse. If one knew where to look, the round face was still visible over the restless sea. There it was—a circle of dark gray, rose-red toward the bottom. It did not shine. It was hard to make out unless he squinted, Tristan found.

The full darkening would last for little over an hour. The tide was just coming in. Tristan strode swiftly across the wet sand. He must make the most of every special moment.

He stopped at the foamy wave edge. Not that he cared whether he got his boots wet, but what he looked for would be hidden by even an inch of water. Especially in such poor light. The waves crashed in. They sloshed over the flat sand till they spent themselves, then slipped back. Tiny objects rolled and came to rest, stranded.

Tristan fixed his attention on the frothy edge of the waves' farthest reach. What had the sea yielded up? Stones and pebbles glistened. Not likely that they were truly pearls, or opals. Certainly there were no diamonds, but each was worth a look.

One skein of foam did not dissolve into the sand. It proved to be a scattering of white pebbles, perfect rounds, ovals and teardrops. Each tiny stone was of breath-catching purity. Tristan collected them carefully and put the precious handful into his sack, deep in a corner for safety.

Thomas was busy trying to catch a ghost crab. He stalked. He pounced. Alas, the crabs could retreat *under* the sand whenever they chose. Thanks to that tactic, the cat had caught nothing yet, and he might not. The difficulty of the hunt did not cause Thomas to abandon it.

Tristan picked up three water-smoothed moonstones, a rough garnet, and a dark green pebble the size of a quail's egg. He found a knot of driftwood shaped like a heart, smooth and white as ivory. All went into the sack.

A hollow glass ball rolled out of a wave and stopped by Tristan's boots. It had escaped from some fisherman's net, perhaps on the far side of the Great Sea. Riding the currents, the float had come to land at last. Wizards saw things in such globes—lost objects, or the misty future. Glass globes were never a match for costly spheres of solid crystal, but they served and were treasured. Blais would be glad of this one. Tristan tucked it inside the front of his pullover.

Polished nuggets of granite offered no hint of any use they might have. But their color was intense. They must be of *some* value. Blais would know. Tristan gathered them too.

Nimble fingers and sharp young eyes, Blais often said. Finding stones of power was the one magical thing Tristan was honestly *good* at. If he gleaned well this night, Blais would be pleased. Possibly pleased enough to reconsider letting him keep Thomas? Tristan thought not. That was nothing to do with him at all, but only with Thomas being a cat.

Thomas had caught a crab. Or else the other way round—the cat gave a sharp squeak as pinchers fastened onto his nose. Thomas clawed the crab loose with both his front paws and tossed it high. The ghost-crab scuttled for safety as it landed, but Thomas pursued it. He played toss-and-catch with the crab several more times, till he came to a large rock jutting out of the sand. Thomas cracked the crab against the rock. Then he set to work getting the crab out of its shell, bite by bite.

Tristan would have considered a crab harvest of his own, but he didn't much care for raw shellfish. Anyway, the crabs were always too quick for him. Thomas had been lucky—or especially stubborn—to catch one.

Something felt warm under Tristan's fingers. That wouldn't be a crab, but Tristan was surprised to find that it was a stone. He scooped damp sand carefully away on both sides. The stone was smooth, but irregularly so. Along one side was a scooped-out spot. It fitted his left thumb as if the scoop had been the fingerskin of a glove. Tristan felt his mouth fall open.

A firestone. There was no doubt of it. He had handled Blais' stone often enough to know what a firestone felt like.

Firestones didn't come from the sea. Not ever. *This* stone must have been carried down to the beach by one of the little streams. Several wound among the dunes when the rains came heavy. Sometimes they reached the sea. Sometimes they were lost under the beach, dwindling away. When they were strong, though, they could carry good-sized stones.

Tristan couldn't make out the stone's color, but he knew it would be gray in daylight, the color of ashes. He walked slowly up the beach. He'd find driftwood at the stormtide line. The folk of Dunehollow collected the cast-up wood, but they never quite got the beach clean. More storm-wrack was forever washing in. Tristan collected a few brittle sticks and laid them carefully across one another.

He turned the firestone about. How did it wish to be held? There would be a correct way, Tristan knew. Blais' stone was notably fussy.

His first instinctive grasp still felt best. The stone wanted his left thumb atop it. Then it rested snugly against his first finger. A second scooped spot there exactly fit his fingertip.

The smooth stone had been born in fire. It still held fire in its heart. That was the warmth he had felt, in the cool sand. He could call that warmth forth. Tristan spoke the words of the spell. As he did, he made summoning passes with his right hand. Words and gestures finished exactly together, and Tristan pointed the stone at the heap of sticks.

Fire shot out of his hand. It licked the driftwood with a sharp *crack!*

Tristan was so startled, he nearly dropped the stone. He closed his fingers hastily around it. Despite the flame, it wasn't hot enough to blister him. The firestone still felt no more than warm.

Tristan scrambled for more wood. He fed the fire carefully until it took proper hold of the fuel. He stared in wonder at the stone in his hand. Usually a firestone yielded a few fat sparks! Blais' stone never put out a tongue of flame. Not even when his master spoke the spell himself.

The firelight made the seacoast seem dark around it. Two green sparks came floating out of the blackness, a handspan above the ground. Thomas blinked approvingly at the fire. He laid down a small fish he'd seized from the shallow surf.

Thank goodness! the cat said. *Cooked food is almost the only worthwhile invention humans can claim.*

Tristan decided that the cat hadn't expected him to be able to provide fire. Tristan chose not to mention that he'd been without the means until quite recently. He got out his brass knife and whispered a honing spell over the blade. In moments Thomas' fish was cleaned, spitted, and well on its way to being roasted.

* * * *

The sky clouded over while they feasted. Tristan didn't care about searching the beach further. He'd already gleaned treasure beyond any of his hopes. No sense being greedy. The hour was late, and now that he was fed, he was drowsy. Tristan walked back to the cottage slowly, carrying Thomas. That turned out to be another thing humans were good for.

* * * *

Tristan felt too weary to bother with the ladder that led to the half-loft. His bed was no more than a nest of blankets on a straw mattress. Plenty of room on Blais' pallet, if he scooped a few books out first. And no ladder. Thomas agreed and hurried to claim a comfortable spot.

Tristan laid his firestone carefully inside a carved wooden box. The box already held a few smooth pebbles, a knotted bit of string and a rainbow-glinting feather—treasures from other expeditions. Tucked into a leather pouch, it could be hung from his belt. Tristan put the pouch under Blais' pillow. As he slept, his fingers kept touch with it, and his dreams were full of wonders.

* * * *

Thomas batted at Tristan's bare toes. Fine sport, till Tristan woke wondering what was pricking his skin. He pulled his feet to safety beneath the blanket, mumbling.

Thomas renewed his attack, liking the challenge, but the thick wool foiled his every effort.

Tristan stretched, then yawned. He'd been out on the beach for much of the night. He had slept less than usual. He might have been groggy, or grumpy, but he felt very well. Indeed, he felt *so* well, so excited and contented both at once, that he could not lie still once Thomas had pestered him awake.

A firestone! Just wait till Blais saw it! At long last he was coming into his power. All his years of hard work and patient study were bearing fruit. The long wait for the harvest would be well worth it, Tristan was certain. He felt as if nothing could ever, *ever* go wrong again.

He lit a fire on the hearth, modulating the spell carefully. No need for streams of fire indoors. He cooked porridge.

Tristan wished wistfully for a bit of bacon, but it had been months since a flitch of it last hung by the chimney. They could really only afford bacon after the autumn hog-butchering.

Maybe there'd soon be more coin on hand for buying a wider variety of food—or more bartering, anyway. Perhaps the farmer who wanted the cabbage-moth spell kept pigs. It was possible. *Anything* was possible, this morning. This *wonderful* morning!

While the porridge bubbled, Tristan fed the cow. He milked her again, then turned her out into the orchard, with a stern warning to chew only the grass. She must not nibble the bark from the young fruit trees. That settled, he went into the coop to let the hens out.

Tristan broke the wards with a flick of his left hand. He bent and pushed the hen-door up, leaning against the spot where it always stuck. Usually the chickens were eager to come out, unless rain was falling.

Today no hens appeared, though the sun shone bright enough. Tristan opened the larger door and went into the coop to chase the hens out. While they were off their nests foraging, he would gather any new-laid eggs. The hens, who preferred to hatch their chicks out, sometimes remembered to object. They got stubborn. They would peck viciously at Tristan's hands if he tried shifting them bodily. The boldest would fly at him. When he'd been smaller, he'd run from the coop to escape them many a morning.

Thomas prudently remained outside the coop, safe from savage hens and misunderstandings. He washed his paws. He combed his whiskers. Tristan did not emerge. Neither did the hens.

Finally, Thomas could stand the suspense no longer. He poked his nose around the corner of the large door, one cautious inch. His whiskers quivered, but he touched nothing.

What smells? he asked, twitching his nostrils.

Tristan made a choking sound, but said nothing. His green eyes were as wide as a human's would go. The expression on his face was strange. Thomas studied him, fascinated. No cat dizzy on fresh catnip looked half so silly. Thomas couldn't imagine what would make a wizard look that way. Not even an apprentice wizard.

He shifted his attention to the interior of the hen house, seeking clues. There were feathers everywhere. They were scattered on the floor and in the nests. A few drifted slowly through the air. More of a mess than even silly chickens usually managed to make, Thomas thought. Red splatters splashed the walls and dappled some of the feathers. Thomas sniffed delicately. *Blood.*

There were bloody tracks too, here and there. The marks were a bit bigger than Thomas' paws. They had not been made by a cat, not even a bobcat or lynx. One plainly showed toenails, a dog's paw print. Thomas sniffed carefully. Dog-family, anyway. *Fox*, he said.

The patient fox had found a way past the wards after all. By the time he had gone out again, not a single hen was left alive inside the coop.

DISASTER

"I don't know what went wrong," Tristan said, too dazed to speak above a whisper. "I set the wards just the way Blais always does." He'd already run through the spell a dozen times, in his mind. He'd called on the strength of the earth, summoned the watchfulness of the moon and the stars, just as he should...

The moon! He hadn't allowed for the eclipse in the formula! Tristan's stomach lurched. He *had* set the wards just as Blais always did. But he should have *adjusted* them instead. How could a dark moon keep watch? And earth alone could not keep out a fox—foxes made their dens in holes dug in that same earth. Foxes knew all of earth's secrets.

Tristan sat down heavily on the edge of a wooden nest-box. He felt sick. Every breath of air stank of old feathers. The coop always smelled nasty to him. Only the chickens could stand it, not having proper noses. Sunlight pouring in through the hen-door quickly heated the small space and made the stench stronger. The coppery reek of spilled blood turned Tristan's stomach. He lurched hastily toward the door.

A big light shape behind one of the boxes caught his eye. Tristan stooped for a better look, his heart thudding in his throat. Was there a survivor?

The pale shape was a chicken. It was the barred hen, the one that always laid the largest eggs. She was limp when Tristan lifted her, and quite dead. The fox had eaten his fill. Then, maybe, he'd carried off a hen for his next meal.

After that he had kept on killing till he ran out of hens. The slaughter was total. That was a fox for you.

Tristan carried the barred hen outside and buried her beneath the arching raspberry canes. She had been a fine egg layer. Hardly his friend, but he could not think of her as meat. When he gathered eggs, she'd always pecked harder than any other hen. However swift his retreat, she'd always gotten him. She'd never abandoned the pursuit till she'd landed at least one blow. Still, she'd been murdered. It didn't make her dinner.

Thomas watched the interment with a solemn expression. After a moment his pink tongue stole out to brush over the tip of his nose. *He* regretted the loss of a chicken dinner. Burying meat struck him as utter foolishness.

Tristan brushed dirt from his hands. The hen was buried. What should he do now? He wanted to be busy. Too busy to think about the disaster he'd caused. He still had a sore spot in the pit of his stomach, though the fresh air was better than the stink inside the coop. He was cold. The sun's warmth didn't seem to touch him.

What were he and Blais to do? The eggs from the hens were often the only fresh food they could count on. The cow was elderly and might go dry any day, despite Blais' spells. They had the orchard and the garden, and Tristan was reasonably good at snaring wild rabbits. Blais traded his charms and medicines for grain and fish—but the chickens were their security. *Had* been.

He'd almost rather the fox had eaten *him*, Tristan thought miserably. Just possibly, Blais would feel the same way. Tristan plodded back toward the cottage, his shoulders slumped. Thomas gave the hen's little grave an appraising look, then sighed and followed the boy. He could always sneak back later. Say under the cover of night.

Tristan spent the morning cleaning out the chicken coop. He scrubbed down the walls. He put piles of bloody feathers into the midden. He shoveled up a year's worth of manure and dug it into the edge of the vegetable patch. He removed the old nests and set the boxes in the sun to air. Work helped him think, distracted him if he got stuck.

His negligence had let the fox get at the hens. There was no escaping that guilt, Tristan decided. There were no excuses. It hadn't been deliberate, but it was his fault nonetheless, whatever Blais might say. It was up to him, therefore, to find a way to replace the birds.

So, just before sun-high, Tristan set off for Mistress Dalzell's cottage.

* * * *

Mistress Dalzell kept chickens. Red and brown hens bustled importantly in her dooryard, bobbing their heads, seeking every sort of beetle and worm. Suspected food not in plain sight was scratched after. A green-tailed rooster strutted about, not so busy overseeing his wives that he failed to notice the cat following at Tristan's heels.

The rooster ran at them with his wings raised, a nasty look in his yellow eyes. Thomas halted. He made himself large, to discourage the rooster. His hair stood on end. His tail fluffed out. He humped his back, flattened his ears, and hissed loudly.

Stalemate. The rooster allowed the cat to pass, but the two kept one another under careful surveillance.

Mistress Dalzell was boiling laundry. A great iron kettle hung over a fire in the side yard. She stirred the pale linens round with a stick, lifting out a bedsheet as Tristan walked the last few feet toward her. He waited politely while she flopped the sheet into the rinse tub. Then—thinking himself very clever—he helped her drape the wet sheet over her drying-line and pegged it down securely for the wind to work on. With two sets of hands, no corner dragged in the dusty yard.

"There's a good lad! Perfect timing!" Mistress Dalzell shoved a wisp of damp hair from her eyes with the back of her left wrist. "Bide just a bit, I'll soon have another one."

Tristan cheerfully lent a hand with the work. Mistress Dalzell's good will was a treasure he intended to catch and hold tight to. When the laundry-boiling was done at last, the woman ducked into her cottage and fetched out a plate of raisin biscuits.

The cakes were rather hard and burnt black on their bottoms, but Tristan was not about to complain. He chewed, swallowed, complimented, and got straight down to business. He would like, he said, to borrow a laying hen.

"One of my hens?" Mistress Dalzell squinted at him. Her eyes reminded Tristan of the raisins, sunk in her face like the dried fruit in the cake dough. "There's not a one of them one bit better than the ones your master has already."

"There was a fox," Tristan confessed.

"Oh dear. *Oh, dear!*" He needed to say nothing more. Foxes were a common plague. "The filthy beast got them all, I suppose?"

Tristan nodded. "What it didn't eat or carry off, it just killed."

"Foxes are murderers, that's what they are." Mistress Dalzell set the empty plate down before Thomas. It held a few black crumbs and a stray raisin. The cat sniffed the offering doubtfully.

"I was thinking," Tristan said, nudging Thomas to remind him to be a polite guest. "That if I might *borrow* a hen for a bit—of course it would take a while to hatch out eggs and raise chicks, but eventually we *would* have a flock again." Thomas nibbled the raisin. "I wouldn't expect a loan just for kindness. I could chop wood for you, as much as you felt was fair. I expect you use quite a bit." Mistress Dalzell took in washing for other folk. If she wasn't washing, then she was dyeing yarn, or lengths of woolen cloth. She needed a fire under the kettle for that, too.

"That lazy son of mine chops wood for me when he comes to dinner." Mistress Dalzell's son did odd jobs of work and mostly spent his pay in the tavern. "He brings me a cartload of driftwood, now and again."

Tristan nodded, understanding. He wasn't discouraged. Surely there was something else he could offer? It was fair to let the owner of the hen set the price. He'd only needed to open the discussion. He could depend upon Mistress Dalzell to keep it going. She understood bargaining.

"I'll tell you what I *would* trade for."

There! The bargaining was under way. Tristan leaned slightly forward, to show his interest.

"Last winter was pitiful hard on bees." Mistress Dalzell nodded her head toward her row of fruit trees. "Three hives I had, and not a one of them thrived. The skeps are empty as can be. I'd trade you eggs for honey. I like a sweet, now and then."

Eggs were *not* a flock of chickens. Eggs were just a few meals, an omelet or a cake. He needed to do better than that, Tristan decided. He tried to choose a suitable counter-offer.

Mistress Dalzell thought of one first. "If you were to bring me a swarm of bees, now—I'd give you a hen for *that*," she said. "I'd like to have bees in my hives again. I've always had my own bees, I have. For years. Honey, and wax to make proper candles. I just had a run of bad luck, what with that sharp winter and then that wet spring. Same as you with the fox."

A swarm of bees? Well, why not? It wasn't as if she was asking him to spin straw into gold, Tristan decided. It was the right time of year for bees to swarm. Healthy hives were becoming crowded, and there were plenty of summer days left for establishing a new hive, before winter killed off all the blossoms and the bees settled into sleep. It might prove to be less work than chopping wood, in the end.

"I'll try," Tristan agreed. "I'll take one of your skeps to fetch the swarm home, if I may?"

FLOWER TO HIVE

You can talk to bees? Thomas asked. The cat tried to sound nonchalant, but his green eyes were wide, missing nothing.

"Well, only a little," Tristan admitted. "Bees really aren't much for conversation."

All that buzzing isn't just their wings? My mother told me it isn't purring. Is it a growling?

"Bees tell each other about the flowers they've visited," Tristan explained. "Over and over, and then maybe over again. That's all that matters to them. Anyway, I needed to find out whether Blais' bees might be thinking of swarming this spring. They aren't." He sighed.

Tristan had lain on his belly in the flowering thyme for most of an hour. It was difficult to have a serious discussion with a bee. The honeybees darted from blossom to blossom and forgot any question that Tristan asked before it was all the way out of his mouth. Those few bees which might be disposed to answer him looked no different from those which were irritable and impatient. Tristan hadn't been stung, but he'd had some close calls. Only wasps were more temperamental. Also, the bees moved constantly, shifting position and trading places among the thyme blossoms. By the time he abandoned his questioning, Tristan had a nasty headache.

Blais' bees were not inclined to swarm anytime soon. That would have been too easy, Tristan supposed. He had a journey ahead of him.

Tristan made himself a small pack. He wrapped up oat-cakes and a bit of cheese, and added a small jar of last year's honey. He wouldn't eat that himself, but he'd need it.

He fetched out his pouch of magic stones from the fireplace shelf and took some dried leaves of bee-balm for making tea. Now that he had his own firestone, he could think about hot drinks. He added a tin cup for brewing the tea.

He'd need a large sack to hold Mistress Dalzell's straw bee skep. Tristan searched through a chest, lifting out stubs of candles, balls of soap, hanks of woolen thread and pack-ets of dried lavender. The empty linen bag lining the bot-tom of the coffer would do nicely.

Tristan didn't want to haul much more along. He might need to walk some distance before he located bees looking for a new home. There was no way to know—he couldn't yet work Blais' scrying bowl. Blais had caught him trying and said he couldn't find the sun on a bright day with the device.

He could live off the country while he searched, though. Better than Jock or Rho either one. Water and firewood were easy enough to come by, when you weren't city-raised. Any bush would be shelter enough for the summer nights, even if rain fell. That and his cloak.

Thomas watched him struggling with the clasp of the threadbare garment. *Aren't you taking some herbs for bee stings?* The cat asked plaintively.

"Swarming bees don't sting," Tristan explained impa-tiently, jabbing his finger as he fiddled with the copper pin. "They don't even eat. The hive sends out scouts, to look for a new home. When they find one, all the other bees stuff themselves with honey. Then they fly with their queen to the new place. They don't feed on the way. They just fly. And they're so full of food, they can hardly stay awake when they stop." He sucked on his finger. "You can handle them all you like, even take the queen out of the swarm. I saw a beekeeper make a beard of bees, at the Dunehollow Fair. He put the queen on his chin, and all the rest of the swarm gathered right around her."

Thomas made a disgusted noise.

"I'm not going to do anything like that," Tristan agreed. "I need to talk to a scout bee."

You need to find one particular sort of bee?

Success didn't sound so likely, put that way. But Tristan refused to be discouraged. Right now, all he needed to do was walk. He could certainly do *that*.

He set the wards around the cottage again. He was *very* careful. He checked and rechecked his work. Then he led the cow along to Mistress Dalzell's. A creature that needed milking twice a day could not be left alone while he went about his quest, wards or no wards. That would be a worse mistake than the chickens. The cow would never forgive him.

* * * *

By sun-high, Tristan was sure the bees he met with would be wild bees. He was a long way from the last cottage he'd seen. That was as it should be. No use his following bees back to some farmer's hive. Even if its bees *did* chance to be swarming, Tristan would not dare take them. Beekeepers always had a fresh skep waiting for swarms. An increase in hives was like an increase in the potato crop. If Tristan helped himself to a swarm, he'd be a thief. He could expect to be treated as such if he was caught. He'd be beaten with sticks, have stones thrown at him, or dogs set on him. The only swarming bees he could safely take were wild ones, bees which belonged to no one save themselves.

That was fine. Wild bees were strong and healthy. Wild bees made good honey, and plenty of it. Mistress Dalzell would like a hardy hive, a hive that could survive the coldest winter.

The sun was hot. Tristan sat down beneath a small tree, grateful for its cool shade. He sipped water from his flask, then chewed an oatcake. Thomas prowled across the meadow, choosing his own lunch. Presently Tristan heard a sharp squeak, but all he could see of Thomas was the cat's lashing tail. Then that settled out of sight. He couldn't see what the cat had captured.

The grass was dotted with scarlet poppies and constellations of white daisies. Broad drifts of clover appeared when the wind brushed the grass, shifting like cloud shadows on the sea. Bees were busy everywhere in the meadow. The air danced with them. A butterfly sailed majestically by. A dragonfly darted after a gnat, performing feats of aerial gymnastics.

As good a place as any to start his search. The woodland beyond the meadow was dense and looked ancient. An old forest held many dead trees. Bees liked the hollows of rotted trunks and branches. Such places made good hive sites. So, now all he needed was to find a bee that was headed for its home.

A bee stayed on a blossom till it had sipped all the available nectar. Then it would shift to a fresh flower. If that blossom had been visited already by another, the bee might not find much to keep it there. Every bee in the field buzzed and bumbled from one flower to another. It was a complicated dance, lacking a fiddler to give the dancers order. How could Tristan choose a single bee and follow it till it was ready to return to its hive? He got dizzy just *thinking* of doing it.

But he could tell when a bee was loaded and ready to depart. Bees took pollen as well as nectar from the flowers. Pollen was food, but it wasn't sucked into a worker bee's stomach. The yellow grains were stored in leg pouches, which swelled as they were filled. Tristan could easily see them on some of the nearest bees, if he leaned close.

Ah! There was such a bee now. It had an orange-gold load upon either hindmost leg. It looked like a tiny donkey bearing panniers. When it rose up, Tristan did likewise, ignoring other bees that his movement startled into flight.

His bee shot off toward the dark band of trees. Tristan tracked its flight for a few seconds. Easy enough! But then he lost the gold speck in the distance, before he could take more than a step in pursuit.

If only bees were as big as dragonflies! Tristan frowned, thinking. If he couldn't follow a particular bee across an open meadow in full daylight, how could he track one through the dark forest? What would Blais suggest? Had he ever read a spell that might help him now?

It wouldn't be a bad thing if the bees were larger—or at least *looked* larger. A round bit of glass could magnify. He should have brought the fishing float he'd found on the beach. But, a drop of water would be every bit as round. Tristan reached for his flask.

He poured water into his palm, then dipped his forefinger. Tristan raised the finger carefully, watching the drop that hung trembling from the tip. He quietly invoked the Principle of Similarity. *Like to like.* What was true for the smaller part would hold for the greater part as well.

Tristan pointed his finger toward a feeding honeybee. He stared at the insect through the drop of water. The bee was wonderfully enlarged. Tristan could count every bristly hair on its fat body. He could see the rainbow facets of its eyes. Those pockets of pollen looked like loaves of bread.

The water drop hung shining in the sun. The bee grew larger, the longer Tristan looked.

"Like to like," Tristan whispered, setting the spell. The bee was *huge*. When it left the flower, he half expected the wind of its churning wings to blow him off his feet.

Distance still made the bee dwindle as it neared the wood, but it appeared to be the size of a small bird. Tristan hurried after the hurtling shape. "Come on, Thomas!" he called to the cat.

The bee was well ahead, but it wasn't flying all that rapidly. Bees were tireless, but hardly falcon-swift. He could keep up, Tristan knew. Thanks to the spell, he could keep the bee in sight. Tristan jogged through the long grass.

All at once, there was no sign of the bee. Tristan stumbled to an uncertain halt. He shaded his eyes against the sun. No use. The only bees he saw were plying their trade in the buttercups around his feet.

Thomas trotted up, raising his tail as he slowed to cover the final few yards. *What's the matter?* The cat asked, not quite out of breath.

Tristan didn't answer. He ran through his herb-lore. The bee must have vanished when something interfered with his spell. But what? Buttercups liked wet feet. Did that mean anything? Tristan stepped forward. Thomas followed, looking cross at being ignored, saying nothing more.

Tristan had to walk fifty yards more, but he found exactly what he expected. A small stream wound invisibly through the long grass of the meadow. "Magic can't cross running water," he told Thomas. "The spell I put on the bee stopped working when the bee flew over the stream."

Oh. Thomas dabbled a paw in the clear water. Shadows darted for cover—minnows or some other tiny, wary fish.

"I'll just have to find another bee after I've crossed," Tristan said, resigned. He looked for a likely spot. The stream was neither wide nor deep, but just too wide to be stepped over easily. He could wade through, but that would soak his boots. He'd rather keep his feet dry, if he could.

The stream sparkled over a bed of golden gravel, no more than ankle deep. That was fine so far as it went, but there might be mud too. Tristan suspected it. If he simply stepped in, he might sink. What he wanted to see were larger stones. He'd step from one to the next and get across. A toppled tree bridging the stream would be fine too. Tristan searched downstream.

He found a nice chain of stones. The only real gap was toward the far bank, and he thought he could jump that bit. If he went fast, he'd have momentum to help him. A heron, fishing upstream, gave Tristan a yellow-eyed glare and stalked away, not concerned enough to bother flying.

Thomas reared up against Tristan's left boot, looking up at him. His wish was obvious—to be carried across. Well, the stream was deep to a cat. Thomas could jump from stone to stone just as Tristan could step, but after his fishing adventure, perhaps he didn't wish to.

Tristan settled the cat on his left shoulder and told him to hold tight. He preferred to have his arms free for balance, not full of cat. The stones looked safe, but crossing water wasn't always simple for wizard-folk.

The first two rocks were flat and dry. The third was evidently round as an egg, under the water. It shifted under Tristan's foot. He left it hastily, but without distress. So long as he didn't linger, small slips were nothing to bother about. If he kept going, he'd be fine. Just like walking on ice.

The next rock was flat, and it didn't shift—but it was moss-covered and slippery as grease. Tristan skidded. He fought hard for his balance, but he lost. Arms flailing, he pitched into the stream.

The water was only a handspan deep, but his landing soaked Tristan from head to heels. Thomas promptly abandoned ship. Digging his claws hard into Tristan's shoulder, the cat sprang toward the bank with all his might. His flight lacked dignity, but he reached the stream's far side dry. That was more than Tristan could claim. He picked himself up and slogged the last few feet, mud sucking fiercely at his boots, water dripping from his hair, his clothes, his chin.

What was that? Thomas gave himself a violent shake, though he had no water in his coat. He licked his shoulder furiously. *Are we joining a circus?*

"Wizards don't cross running water any better than their spells do," Tristan admitted. His shoulder stung. Thomas' claws had pierced his skin as well as his clothes.

Next time, you're on your own. Thomas had recovered his dignity, but he was in no mood to forgive.

"All right." Absently, Tristan picked up a water-smoothed piece of slate. The stone was a perfect oval, of a deep, uniform color. Tristan could feel the magic in it, though either crossing the water or falling had left him dizzy and unsettled. He climbed the low bank, sat on a fallen tree, and dragged his boots off.

No drying-spell for him *this* time! The sun ought to be up to the job. It wouldn't need to work hard this time—he wasn't soaked down to his skin. And maybe by the time he was dry, his heart would have settled back down where it belonged, instead of banging away in his throat till it was all Tristan could do to breathe around it. He hated running water, if he had to cross it!

Thomas stalked a scarlet dragonfly. The dragonfly contemptuously stayed just out of his reach. Yellow sunlight poured down. After a few moments, Tristan put his boots back on. He filled his flask from the stream—might as well get fresh water while he had the chance. There was plenty of it. Repeating the drop-charm on another bee, he set off again.

He lost this bee too. The stream wound considerably. Possibly there was more than *one* stream. It was hard to see, in the tall grass. At least, hard to see very far ahead.

The sun was sinking when he reached the edge of the wood. Soon there was not a bee to be seen anywhere. Tristan gathered dry sticks while looking about for shelter. A bush would do, if he found nothing better. The low-hanging branches of a fir could be both roof and walls.

Tristan was prepared to spend a night or two in the open. The sky was clear, rain unlikely. He had food to eat, wood for a fire, a firestone to light the blaze. He had Thomas for company. Most wild animals would have no interest in him. All was well.

He refused to be discouraged. Swarming bees weren't common. They weren't scarce either. Patience and persistence would pay off in the end. Tristan watched the golden flames dancing, searing a small fish he'd hooked from the nearest bit of stream. He wasn't worried. Not in the least. He was a wizard in training. Night held few terrors for him.

He would accomplish his chosen quest. Only he must be fairly quick about it. He had to be back at the cottage before Blais returned. Ideally, with the matter of the chickens well in hand. The flames began to take the shapes of hens and roosters as he thought about that.

Blais might be away for more than a week. He *had* been known to visit with Master Sedwick for the best part of a month. They were great friends. But it wasn't likely Blais would be gone so long this time—there was that spell for the cabbage moths. Blais would have dealt with it before he left, had he intended to be long away.

There were stars in the tiny bits of sky visible between the trees. No moon appeared, at least not before Tristan settled himself for sleep. He felt it ought to have risen, and he wondered hazily if the sky was clouding after all. Would there be rain? Probably the trees would keep it off of him. Thomas curled on his chest, warm as a stove and purring. Tristan forgot the moon. He was asleep well before his thoughts spun themselves out.

THE BOG

Entering the wood, Tristan kept a sharp eye out. He expected nothing. There were few flowers and no honeybees. A dark bumblebee lumbered past, making noise enough for a whole swarm. Bumblebees nested alone, in holes in the earth. They made no honey, so far as Tristan knew.

He studied the birds he saw carefully. Birds often knew quite well where honey was to be found. He had read of them leading bears to hives, so as to have the scraps after. Tristan hoped there were no bears in the wood. He wasn't the meal of choice for such a big, slow creature—but one never knew. He walked from clearing to clearing, along trails probably made by deer. He used his ears as well as his eyes—the hum of thousands of wings would give a bee-tree away.

When Tristan came out of the trees and back into grassland, he found flowers once more, and bees tending the blossoms. He found running water again, too. It was like a plague—a plague of streams. He couldn't follow a bee more than a few hundred yards, which wasn't far enough. Trying a log that proved wobbly, he fell into another stream and found a minnow in his pocket. With a sigh, he threw the fish back into the water.

Another toppled trunk held a beehive in its empty heart. Tristan observed it from a little distance, his heart beating fast. The bees took no notice of him. They were numerous, but without choking the air, busily content. Plenty of flowers bloomed within easy flight.

Tristan sighed and turned away. There was no reason for the bees to be seeking a new home. No suggestion of his was likely to influence them into swarming. And his feet hurt.

Tristan stuffed his boots with moss, but that didn't help for more than a few minutes. Trouble was, his feet were soaked. The ground was wet, even when he wasn't struggling to cross yet another inconvenient stream. Tristan looked around, frowning. Watching his feet, he'd lost sight of his surroundings.

The carpet of grass tended more to mounds and heavy clumps. The spaces between the clumps reflected the blue sky. Where there had been drifts of clover, now Tristan saw great stands of water-loving yellow flag.

Grassland had given way to bog. The place drained poorly—in fact, a great deal of water drained *into* the area, judging by the streams. Trying to keep his feet dry forced Tristan to walk twisty courses. He might have been caught in a maze with walls of glass. He was not confined, but he could not go where he wished. The land led him between ribbons of water.

Mostly that water was no more than an inch deep. But it lay over mud which was often far deeper. There were pools too, probably deep enough to drown a horse. Those looked little different from the shallow spots, but an ill-considered step proved the difference. The air was thick with insects, most of which bit. Plainly, they found human blood a tasty meal.

Tristan would have turned back—but bees were as plentiful as the mosquitoes. Bog plants bloomed and blossomed, just the same as their dryland kin. Bees didn't need to walk. They needn't swim. Wherever there were flowers, a buzzing, shifting dance of fuzzy nectar-gatherers filled the air. The bloodsuckers didn't bother *them*.

Tristan slapped the back of his neck, then stared unhappily at the blood smeared across his fingers. Where would bees nest in this place? If he thought about it, he should be able to see the answer. It certainly wouldn't be close to the ground, like the last hive. But bees still favored trees.

When the bog had been drier country than it presently was, trees had grown far from the forest edge. Drowned now, those ancient trunks still stood, like sentries never relieved at their posts. The dead snags could be seen for considerable distances through the heart shimmer and insect clouds. They could well hold bees. They looked ideal.

Reaching them, that was another matter entirely. The bog never allowed Tristan two steps in a single direction. Dodging and swatting hungry bugs only made matters worse. Tristan soon gave up any hope of actually remembering his course. Retracing it would be like following a mouse's scurryings.

Going back, he'd simply have to do the best he could. Or whatever the bog would allow. He couldn't be lost as long as he could see the forest, Tristan decided. A shrill whine beside his ear made him jerk sharply to one side. His feet wandered into a mudhole. Mired to his knees, Tristan swatted at the most persistent pests. He'd be bled white by nightfall, if he didn't do something!

After a moment's thought, he began to mutter an incantation. Thomas sprang onto his shoulder, startling him so that Tristan had to begin his spell over again.

What's it do? The cat asked.

"Hopefully, it keeps these flying needles off me before I run out of blood!" Tristan started over yet again.

Maybe three repetitions did the trick. Suddenly, the warding began to work. Fewer bugs landed on him, and most of them took off again in haste. Only the boldest dared torment him, and putting the hood of his cloak up fended them off. Dragging his feet out of the muck, Tristan struggled onward.

A bee zipped past his left ear, well ahead of Thomas' darting paw. Another shot by on the right. Tristan thought he saw a pattern to the two flights. He had, after all, been right about those drowned trees. One of them held a bee-hive.

As he closed in on the bee-tree, Tristan saw that the air around it was full of bees. The hive had at least three entrances, and a shifting cloud of bees surrounded each one. As Tristan's approach was noted, the activity increased. Tristan halted. He felt Thomas go tense on his shoulder.

The cat was right to be nervous. If they ventured too near, the warrior bees would emerge to drive them off. This was a great hive, a city of wings. Its citizens would know how to deal with a honey-thief. And who would dare the bog, save a robber?

Tristan found a dry spot and sat down. There were no flowers near him, but bees began arriving at once. They inspected him, flying past and around and over him. The air hummed. Slowly, Tristan opened his pack. He took out the jar of amber honey. He put a single drop on the tip of his tongue. Then he spoke a word of power and swallowed.

The honey reminded his stomach that it was empty, but he hadn't come all the difficult way to eat. Tristan dipped his finger again. He rested his elbow on his knee, so that his finger was on a level with his eyes. Then, he simply waited for a bee to accept his invitation to parley.

Soon enough, a bee arrived. She scented the honey, a stronger lure than the most fragrant flower. She circled once, shining golden in the sun, then made a dainty landing on Tristan's hand. Her antennae twitched. Her mouth dipped toward the honey. She sipped at it.

The honey still on his own tongue sealed a magical bond between them. *Hello,* Tristan said, friendly and polite. He watched the bee.

She wiggled her striped abdomen, as if his greeting had startled her. She made no move to sting him, though. Tristan was careful not to move. He did not so much as blink. Polite and harmless. She'd die if she stung him, and he'd have to start over with another bee, at a great disadvantage. And in pain, surely.

Greetingzzzz, the bee replied. *Thizzz izzz eggzzzellent honey.*

Good flowers, Tristan explained. *Fruit tree blossoms and every sort of herb.*

Thomas had a dance of bees about him. The cat sat calmly, but his eyes darted like minnows. The tip of his tail twitched, as if Thomas could not keep it still no matter how he tried.

Tristan hoped the cat could at least keep his *paws* still. Swatting a curious bee would not make a good impression. Surely Thomas understood that?

He returned his attention to the bee standing on his finger. *This is a busy hive,* Tristan said. *Your queen must be mighty.*

His guest wiggled her antennae at him. *Buzzzzy, yezzzz. Szzzzzip many flowerzzzz. Szzzoon we go.*

He could *feel* her speech, vibrating on his fingertip. Her tiny feet felt impatient. She was tapping four of them at once. *Soon you go?* he asked. *To a new home? Your queen is leaving?* If a new queen was hatched, the old took many of the workers and sought a new home.

Szzzztrong, izzzzz sheeee. Szzzztrong. The bee's fur was the color of honey, rich and warm. *Szzzoon we go,* she repeated.

Yes, I can see there's no room here. Tristan nodded at the tree. *So many bees.*

Squeezzzzzed, are we! The bee danced, very gracefully, on all her six feet. Excited. Eager. Small wonder. Swarming was a great adventure, and it did not come in most bees' short lifetimes. This one would be elderly in a month's time.

How do you seek a new home? Tristan asked. Slowly, he put out another drop of honey. Like offering a neighbor another cup of tea, to keep useful gossip flowing. He'd watched Blais do just that.

Honey was far richer than nectar. Bees fanned nectar with their wings, concentrating it. Rather, Tristan thought, like men making wine from the thin juice of new grapes. His bee rubbed her wings together with delight at what he gave her.

Szzzend scoutzzzz, she told him, sipping. *Find new placezzzzzz.*

With many flowers, Tristan agreed. *Clover and harebell. Clary and lavender and coltsfoot. Apple and pear, plum and apricot and brambleberries. Wild thyme by the acre.*

Exzzzzellent, she said, approving the menu.

Hard to come by, Tristan told her sadly. *I've just walked through those woods. The meadows are a long way back, the clover blossoms and the red poppies. The trees are done blossoming. Nothing but leaves now, in the forest.*

Thizzzzz? The bee asked, tapping an antenna at the honey smeared on Tristan's finger. As canny as a goodwife confronting a peddler.

I carried it with me, Tristan said. *Not from the woods, no. From the place I came from. I'm going back there, soon.*

Szzzzoon?

In the morning, Tristan said.

She sampled the honey again. *Tazzzzty.*

Good flowers, Tristan repeated. *But not enough bees. I hoped to fetch a few back. If I found a hive ready to swarm. Ready for an adventure.*

She buzzed, too excited for human words. *Uzzzzz?* he heard at last.

If you like. Tristan wanted to smile, but wasn't sure she might not misunderstand. Bees had no teeth, but bears certainly did.

I will azzzzk! Many flowerzzzzzzz?

Many flowers, Tristan confirmed.

The bee took off, circled Tristan's head, and landed once more. She gathered information as her sisters did nectar and pollen. A bit here, a bit there. *Izzzzz far?*

Well, far enough. Maybe too far for a swarm to fly, but that wasn't a problem. I can help you. Tristan showed her the skep, carefully. *You could all ride this way, you and your queen, all the workers. No rain to worry about. No birds.*

Birdzzzz szzzzeek uzzzzz?

Maybe he shouldn't have mentioned birds. Birds could easily penetrate the bog. *No birds. You would ride, safe. Secret. Until you come to your new home.*

She danced in the air, looping loops, tumbling sideways. *Stzzzzzzzzzay. I will azzzzzzk.* She shot straight away, so rapidly that Tristan's eyes could not follow the straight flight. He blinked several times.

Thomas had a bee on the tip of his nose. The cat stared cross-eyed at it and sneezed as it left him. *Smooth enough for a merchant,* he commented. *Perhaps wizardry isn't your best calling.*

Tristan was busy putting more honey on his finger. He set the jar down open before him. He expected numerous guests soon.

A little cloud issued from the tree. The air was loud with bee wings.

Tristan knew his bee at once. She landed first, for one thing. Already accustomed to him, she was unafraid. The others held back briefly before joining her. All sipped, some on Tristan's finger, the others from the rim of the honey jar. He could tell they agreed on the quality of the sample.

Good flowerzzz!

Good flowerzzzz! The bees exclaimed the compliment over and over, like wedding guests singing a round-song.

Orchards, Tristan explained again. *Vegetable plots and herb beds. Crop fields. Pastures of clover. All handy to the hive.*

Man's crops were thick-sown, unlike the random plantings of nature. Luxurious. The bees were all dancing now, imagining the riches Tristan spoke of. He let them inspect the skep of coiled straw. They quickly found the tiny door.

Szzzzmall, one bee complained. Her chorus was taken up by the rest. *Szzzzzmallllllll!*

Szzzzmall, Tristan's bee agreed mournfully.

It's only for the journey, Tristan assured her. *Your home will be much larger. Room in it for many combs of honey, many brood combs. And an apple tree to shade it.*

Apple blozzzzzomzzzzz? There was more dancing.

Every spring, Tristan promised. He did not recall passing any wild apple trees as he went through the wood, but there must be some. These bees seemed to consider apple blossoms treasure—or legends. He must be sure to mention them often.

Izzzzz time, a darkish bee announced. The bees formed into a circle, their antennae tapping and touching. Those bees which had been longest at the honey jar bumbled a trifle and were slow to find their places. The circle hummed. Then all at once it took wing and headed for the great hive.

Did they accept? Thomas sniffed at the jar.

"I don't know. I think they went to azzzk." Tristan shook his head sharply. "*Ask.* Those must have been the scouts, the ones charged to find a new home, and guide the swarm to it." A few bees still flew around him, and the jar, but these were shy. They'd be the common workers, content to remain in the great hive with the new queen.

Tristan carried the skep to a dry, flat spot nearer the bee tree. Carefully, he unwrapped a comb of honey and tucked it inside, at the very center of the skep. Bees gorged on honey before they swarmed. They would not forage on their way to a new home. A queen, though, could not be allowed to go hungry. He must offer her the best he had on hand. That was only sense. And good manners. She *was* a queen.

Soon she came, in royal state. Queens flew only to mate and to swarm. The royal wings might be spread no more than twice in her entire life. The queen's attendants surrounded her. Nothing must trouble the ruler on her stately progress. Had the skep not been to hand, the living bodies of thousands of bees would have raised a wall about their queen whenever she rested. They flew in a crowd all about her. From the instant she hatched, she had never been alone.

The queen alighted at the entrance of the skep. She could not be mistaken for one of her worker children—she was far larger than any of those, or her attendants. Her abdomen by itself was longer than a whole bee. The queen—and the queen alone—laid every one of the eggs for the hive. Her own weight in eggs, each and every day. Every worker, every nurse, every scout and soldier and courtier was her child. She was surrounded now by her offspring, all of them buzzing continual concern for her health and her comfort. The queen's court trailed behind her into the skep.

Heralded by loud buzzing, a thick stream of workers followed. They were orderly and not much excited. All workers knew was nectar-gathering, which did not require imagination.

Last of all came the scouts. As the first was following the workers into the skep, another circled Tristan's head in greeting.

Many flowerzzzzz! She buzzed excitedly. Then she too darted into the skep.

CIRCLES

With the swarm clustered inside it, the skep felt heavy. Tristan opened the linen bag wide and carefully set the skep upon it.

He used the bag's drawstrings to gently close the top over the straw cone. Best to carry the bees so. The bag would shield the swarm from sun and rain. The darkness inside it would keep the bees calm. He could feel the workers within shifting into their places about their queen. Their buzzing was a purr, louder than a cat's. There were more lives in the bag than Tristan could ever count, even if they were all small lives.

He set off, retracing his path. At least, Tristan supposed he did. It was hard to be sure. So far out in the bog, he couldn't see any edge of woodland—tall grass got in the way. Tristan put the bee-tree at his back. After all, he had certainly walked straight toward it, coming in.

As if one *could* walk straight, in the water-maze of the bog. Tristan was turned this way and that as he sought sound footing. He wasn't troubled for his own comfort—bees would appreciate a dunking even less than Thomas had.

He did not expect familiar sights. The bog paths weren't full of landmarks. He wouldn't come upon any of his own tracks. The sucking mud swallowed footprints the instant his boots left them.

Tristan didn't reckon to be sure of his way—not every single step of it. He held a general course. He didn't know *where* he'd emerge from the bog, but he had no doubt that he *would* emerge.

So, being lost came as a total surprise.

After half an hour of stepping from one grass tussock to another, Tristan glanced back over his shoulder. He couldn't see the bee-tree. The light was failing, running out of the sky as night seeped in.

No doubt that was why he couldn't see the forest ahead of him. The gory light of sunset glinted orange and apricot on the water of the bog. The bog plants, the iris and the reeds and the sedges, were all black as coal dust, spikes that were differenced only by their heights.

We won't be out of this by dark, Thomas said helpfully. His paws were wet, and the cat hated that. Playing in the water was one thing. Being trapped by it was quite another matter.

"Sky's clear enough." Not even a rag of cloud overhead. "There ought to be a moon, later. It's only a couple of days off full. Plenty of light then."

If he aimed himself straight at the moonglow on the horizon, he could keep a steady course, Tristan decided. He wasn't certain where that course might take him, but at least he wouldn't wander in a circle. The need to watch the ground just in front of his feet made it hard to keep from straying. If he walked in a broad arc, he'd wind up where he'd begun. Tristan was on his guard against that, but still it could happen. The bog had few landmarks, even by day. Tall as he was, he couldn't see far enough. One pool looked just like the next and the last. Every tussock of grass mimicked its neighbor. The sky over all looked infinite.

Nightsong replaced the day's insect buzz. Frogs were the singers—frogs of every size, by their voices. Tristan heard shrill pipings, deep boomings, croakings pitched everywhere between. He stepped over to a dry hillock.

Possibly it was an abandoned muskrat lodge. Tristan sat down and waited for moonrise. Once he'd been still for a bit, the nearest frogs regained their boldness, and added their voices to the distant choir.

Stars came out in the deep purple sky. He ought to be able to use some of them for guides, Tristan knew. Yet stars did shift with the hours. And stars wouldn't give him light enough to pick his way in such country. Best to wait for the moon.

Waiting, Tristan grew drowsy. His day had begun early. It had been long. The sun had been hot. He'd walked many a league, even if never in an especially straight line. Trudging through the sucking mud of the bog was tiring. And negotiating with bees sapped whatever strength he might have had left.

Tristan rested his head on an upraised knee. Only for a moment, he promised himself. Too long, and he'd have a stiff neck. But just for a moment, to rest…

* * * *

His eyes were gritty. For a dozen heartbeats, Tristan was utterly at a loss. He couldn't decide where he was. He didn't remember how he'd come to be there. The darkness, the lack of familiar objects about gave the feel of a dream. He wanted to wake up, but he wasn't sure he was asleep.

He lifted his head—and pain shot through his neck. The discomfort convinced him that he was awake. But awake where? Where was he?

Memory came back. The bees. The bog.

If he'd slept past moonrise…if he'd lost his only guide through his own weakness…Tristan's mouth was dry. How *stupid*, to fall asleep!

No. There it was! A golden-pale glow on the horizon. Tristan got to his feet, dizzy with relief. He fumbled with the strap of the linen bag.

Frogs went silent as he moved. In the sudden quiet, he could hear the bees humming inside the skep. Had he disturbed them? No. Bees used the beating of their many wings to warm the hive in cool weather, on chill nights. Motion made heat. Rub your hands together, soon your fingers were warm. Bees were clever. And these sounded comfortable.

A pair of green coins shone, hovering midway between Tristan's toes and his knees. That would be Thomas, otherwise invisible.

Moon's up? the cat asked.

Tristan nodded and settled the strap on his shoulder, so the skep rode on his back. No jostling, not joggling. The bees made no protest.

Not much light, Thomas complained.

"There's probably a little mist. It should be brighter as the moon climbs higher." Tristan peered out across the bog, trying to sort water from muddy earth. He could fix a course on the rising moon, but he'd still have to watch his feet closely. Some bogs fringed lakes. He could be at the edge of one such now, for all he knew.

Taking frequent bearings on the moonglow, Tristan slogged off. Was the moon rising over a hill, or behind trees? It was slow to climb, meaning the horizon was not flat, or bare. There was something tall out there. Earth, or the forest edge. At this distance, he had no way to decide. Tristan was content if he was only in mud up to his ankles, rather than his knees.

The frogs grew used to his splashing and kept up their singing no matter what Tristan did. Obviously he was no raccoon hunting a supper of tender frogs. A raccoon would have made *far* less noise than he did.

Odd, how the night stretched. Tristan was certain he had walked for the best part of an hour. Yet in such a time the moon would surely have lifted clear of the highest hill. It would be lighting his way from overhead. He looked for it.

Toadstools! How had he wandered so far off his course? Instead of straight ahead, the glow was well to his right.

Tristan corrected his aim. His feet ached with cold and wet. His calves cramped. His knees were sore and his hips hurt. The mud was hard to avoid. By day, the color of the plants had told him where to step. Bright green was the shade to be wary of—that was usually duckweed, which grew lushly over standing water. But in the dark, every color was some shade of gray. Unless it was black. Tristan's steps were unsteady and often quite deep.

He was off course *again.* Tristan bent his steps to his right, determined to cease his straying. He was not a child, to constantly lose his way. He was a wizard in training. He knew better than to walk in circles. Was the load on his shoulder subtly steering him awry?

He soon had Thomas on the other shoulder to balance the load. Wading through water by day *and* night did not suit the cat. Tristan didn't blame Thomas one bit. His own longer legs were no real advantage. Nor was stopping to rest a temptation. Whenever Tristan stood still, he began to sink.

Thomas wasn't heavy, but his shifting about was annoying. Tristan didn't object to the purring. Warm fur against his neck made a nice contrast to the chill wet paws that kept bumping his ear. Had Thomas settled and stayed put, he'd have been a pleasure to carry.

However, it seemed the cat couldn't decide how he wished to ride. Thomas turned this way, that way. He used his claws freely, to secure his position. Thomas kept his claws wonderfully sharp. Their tips could pierce skin right through several layers of heavy cloth. Tristan gasped and took a distracted step straight into deep water.

Floundering, trying not to jostle the bees, Tristan got his footing back at last. He faced the pale glow once more. Would the moon *never* rise?

Which one's the moon? Thomas asked, shifting about once more.

"There's only *one* moon!" Tristan snapped, shoving Thomas' tail out of his eyes. If only the cat would stay still! Tristan raised his shoulder to protect his neck from straying claws, but that just made Thomas shift again.

There are two glows. Which is the moon?

"What?" Tristan halted. He began to sink into the mud at once. He kept moving because he was forced to, but he looked sharply over his shoulder. Thomas' whiskers brushed his cheek, like a spider's legs.

One over there. And another there. Thomas tapped a paw against Tristan's cheek, asking him to turn his head. *Not to mention that they move.*

Tristan's feet stumbled onto firmer ground. He wished his wits could do the same. Thomas was right. There *were* two glows. And neither one of them rose as the moon should long since have done.

The wet earth seemed willing to bear him for a moment. Tristan took a careful look at the sky. The stars were sharp enough. He couldn't see even the thinnest veiling of cloud. Once he sorted out a constellation or two, he'd have his direction.

Then he saw the moon.

The near-disk was gray as old iron. A wash of rusty color along its lower edge helped that resemblance along. It was far above the horizon. In fact, it was well overhead. Tristan had to tip his head back to see it. No great wonder that he hadn't noticed it rising. The moon was still as dim as it had been during the eclipse.

How odd. Tristan couldn't remember ever seeing such a moon on a clear night.

The light he'd been following—just possibly he'd been following *both* the lights, at one time or another, Tristan thought dizzily—must be a marsh-light. *Dead-lights,* some folk named them. They were said to lure unwary travelers to deep muddy graves.

Well, these had not managed to do that to him, but it was hardly for want of trying. Tristan decided to stay where he was till dawn. It wouldn't be so comfortable as the muskrat lodge had been, but he might not find another dry spot in the darkness. He couldn't keep wandering through the mud all night. He'd be all right once the sun came up. There would be no mistaking the *sun.*

The dead-lights flitted about, seeking to recapture his attention. Tristan ignored them. *If only he had a place to sit!* His feet hurt, but he dared not set the skep down, far less himself. The ground underfoot was just too wet. Thomas began to seem very heavy on his left shoulder. Standing for the remainder of the night was not a happy prospect. He was *so* tired.

It could be worse. He *could* be in mud to his neck. Tristan sighed and, for lack of anything better to do, watched the dead-lights. When he had tired of that, he turned slowly in place and watched the other way for a while. Moving should help him keep warm, same as the bees. He examined the stars. He tried to reckon how many hours remained till morning. He knew when certain stars should rise...

There was a third light out there. Tristan squinted at it. The brightness lacked the faint green cast of the dead-lights. It shone silver as the moon *should* have, only it was on the ground, not sailing across the sky. Or so it seemed. In the gloom, his eyes tried to invent explanations for anything they could not plainly see.

The longer he watched the light, the more Tristan wanted to know just what it was. It always held steady, as if whatever made it was fixed to the distant spot. Was it starlight reflected from a pool of water? It seemed too bright for that. Could it be pale flowers? Tristan didn't think so. He hadn't seen anything of that sort when there'd been light to see it by. Most flowers shut themselves at night. Closed their petals tight till morning.

The mud gave off sucking sounds. The sounds continued whether Tristan moved or stood still. It sounded like something strolling past, invisible. Tristan shivered at the thought. He told himself sternly that the notion was pure nonsense.

Just then, Thomas dug several claws deep into his shoulder. Tristan gasped. He was certain that he heard something—*not* Thomas—snicker at him.

Tristan willed himself to relax. He lowered his shoulders. He unclenched his fists. He struggled to swallow his stomach back down, to forget that his mouth was dry. He was long past being afraid of the dark. He was a *wizard.* Well, he was an apprentice wizard. But he was past such childish fears. Definitely past them.

Something darted past the tail of his eye.

Tristan couldn't tell what it was. He turned so fast that he nearly fell, but he saw nothing. He *heard* another thick chuckle. It might have been a bubble of swamp gas bursting on the surface of the bog. Or not. The hair on the back of his neck lifted.

Just to help matters along, Thomas made a weird noise, low in his throat. His throat was just beside Tristan's left ear.

"Can you see it?" Tristan hissed.

Yesss.

The cat did not say what he saw. He didn't need to. Plenty of nasty things haunted certain bogs by night. *Moonless* nights were their favorite times. And that faded moon overhead was useless.

Tristan reached a decision, without knowing whether he'd been seeking one.

"Whatever it is, it's too bold. If this place weren't so *wet*—I can't set wards here. Let's go over to that light."

Think it's dry there?

There was no way to know. At least the steady light wasn't the color of the dead-lights. Tristan splashed off. Something splashed behind him. Tristan told himself that it was only his imagination. He refused to look back over his shoulder.

He wanted to recite a spell that would firm his footing, or keep his boots dry. Only the driest thing in the bog was his throat. He couldn't speak. He couldn't swallow. He *definitely* heard something behind him.

Tristan's heart thumped violently in his chest. If he opened his mouth to whisper a spell, it would probably fly right out.

Whichever way he turned, his back was unprotected. Tristan's skin itched, and not just where Thomas' claws were digging in. He felt constantly watched.

The frogs went silent. In their place, the bog bubbled to itself. The mud made nasty smacking sounds, like rubbery lips kissing. What could it be? Tristan had seen nothing. Therefore, *anything* might be hidden in the night. Tristan faltered, longing to run. He resisted the temptation. He must not give way. If he panicked, he'd be herded like a sheep by whatever was back there. He'd be drowned long before morning light. He must be calm.

Walk. Walk *slowly.* Never look back.

Look at the light, Thomas suggested into his ear.

The cat was right. Looking at the light was better. It was nearer than it had been. At least *it* wasn't playing hide-and-seek with him, the way the dead-lights had. Tristan's steps brought him closer to it, not quickly, but visibly.

And the ground *must* be drier—Tristan saw the black shapes of trees. *Dead* trees, *drowned* trees, but *trees,* all the same. He'd be able to hang the bee skep from one of those branches. His back wouldn't ache so, if he could get a little relief from the weight.

The white glow was behind the tangle of bare branches. It shifted in place, moved forward, to and fro. Tristan squinted. He took another step. He halted. His lips parted as his mouth opened. His whole face went slack with wonder.

A pale creature crouched behind the interlaced wood, feet braced, head down. Its long mane bound it in place. The silken hairs were caught on the rough branches, knotted and twisted dozens of times. Snared so, all it could raise toward Tristan was its eyes.

Save for the eyes, it was as white as the moon. Its hide glowed with pearly light. By its shape and size, it might have been a pony, strayed somehow into the bog.

Except for the single horn sprouting from the center of its wide white forehead, spiraling toward an icicle point between its cloven hooves.

THE UNICORN

The unicorn's beauty was overwhelming. Tristan could not move. Not his feet, not his hands. He could not breathe. He could not remember that he *needed* to breathe. He could only stare, astonished.

The unicorn stared back at him, fiercely. Ensnared though it was, helpless, it warned Tristan to keep his distance. Its dark eyes were deep and ancient as the spaces between the stars overhead. While he looked into them, Tristan felt awe and more than a little dread. He stayed where he was. He held his breath.

The horn between the eyes was as long as his arm, but very slender. It tapered. It twisted along its length, and every ridge of it glinted a different color. Tristan had seen no colors since the sun had set with a last flaunt of glorious banners. Now he discovered salmon, peach, rose, palest lavender and a green nearly white. Sparks of blue and gold accented the pure hues. The crowns of kings never held such jewels.

That wonderful horn was jammed under what must have been a root, while the drowned tree was living. A dark pool of water glittered under the tangle. It looked a little like a well. Maybe the unicorn had been tricked into gazing at its reflection, lured into a trap. Tristan had read that mirrors fascinated the beasts. Maybe it had simply lowered its head to drink.

However it had happened, the horn was stuck tight. Tristan remembered getting his hand caught inside on of

Blais' herb jars once. The hand had gone in easily. Out was quite another matter. In the end, Blais had smashed the jar to free him.

The unicorn had obviously struggled. One cloven hoof was snared by another twisty root. The silken mane was caught fast on the tree, strand after strand after strand. Every movement the unicorn made had only bound it more securely. Now, it could scarcely stir. It rocked back and forth, but not strongly enough to tear free. The unicorn was helpless. It was frightened. It was furious.

The bog-haunts had tricked it, Tristan decided. He hung the skep on a handy branch. Then he began setting wards against visitors. He couldn't work magic upon running water, but earth—even soggy earth ringed round by a great deal of water—was another matter.

Tristan was startled to see that his fingers left trails of silver in the air. The traces of his spellcasting faded slowly away as he stared. They were useful, he decided nervously. He could *see* the protections he was shaping, instead of having to hold his objective in his head in the usual way. That was an advantage, for all it took some getting used to. Once the protective circle was complete, Tristan turned back to the unicorn.

How long had it been trapped here? It had been bold enough to confront him, when he might have been a danger. But now it drooped. It looked somehow shrunken. It closed its eyes. Exhausted, was it? Maybe it had been caught a *long* while. It seemed worn out.

Tristan laid a spell on his brass-bladed knife, to make the tip sharp. Later, when he set to work against the tree, he might need the knife to sprout teeth. Whatever it took to free the creature slumped against the tree, he would do.

First, Tristan sorted out the mane. Silver hair rippled over his fingers like silk, as he pulled strand after strand away from the rough bark. He used the knife's tip to widen narrow cracks in the wood. Forcing the knife in, he held the cracks open while he released the strands they'd trapped. The unicorn twisted its head sideways, testing new limits of motion. The horn was still stuck fast.

"I'll get to that," Tristan assured the creature. He spread two branches that had trapped a hoof, ignoring a third that had nothing to do with the capture. The wood barely yielded. Tristan had to push with all his strength, and the angle was awkward. Holding the branches, he nudged the unicorn's leg with his shoulder. "Pull it out!" he gasped, hoping it would understand him.

The unicorn shied back from his touch. The silver hoof slipped free. Its edge grazed Tristan's chest. The roots promptly closed upon Tristan's fingers.

The blow was sharp enough to bruise, almost enough to crack bone. Tristan put his knuckles into his mouth, holding back a groan. He waited for the pain to ebb. The unicorn's flailing hooves showered him with sand. The creature struggled wildly, uselessly. Nothing held it now but the horn. That, however, held it securely.

"Calm down," Tristan told it. "Stop thrashing. That's what got you stuck in the first place, I bet."

The spirals of the horn seemed to have meshed with the twists of the roots. The roots couldn't have grown around the horn—though they looked as if they had. Roots didn't grow that fast. Tristan studied the problem from a little distance. He couldn't go too close. If he did, the unicorn began to pull back in a panic. It kicked sand into his eyes, and then he couldn't see. Tristan let it settle, twice and thrice. Its silver sides heaved like a smith's bellows. The sound of its breathing was harsh.

The unicorn was scared. It was desperate. It might, for all Tristan knew, die from the shock of being held captive.

His fingers ached. They had begun to swell. Working magic was going to be difficult soon, Tristan thought sickly. He squinted at the damage. He'd better free the creature *now*, while he still could. He put both hands on the horn, ignoring the cloud of sand which quickly surrounded him. He held on tight.

Tristan's palms tingled. His swollen fingers throbbed. That might only be from trying to close them tightly. The unicorn's breath came in hot puffs. Its eyes were circled with white, frantic. Its mouth opened wide. It snapped its teeth, but it couldn't get near enough to bite him.

"Steady," Tristan told it. He kept his right hand on the horn. He slid the left down to investigate the roots. The glow of the horn gave him some light. Not that he especially needed to see. He could *feel* the tension at the spot where the horn was caught. He could tell which roots it merely passed under and which were locked fast upon it.

The horn was caught in two places, nearly a hand's width apart. "Stop struggling," Tristan ordered the unicorn. "You could snap your horn, I think." The horn might grow back, but he had no way to know whether it would.

A wonder it hasn't. Thomas had come close. The cat peered intently at the root. *What are you going to do?*

"Pry the roots apart." Tristan worked his knife tip in again, very close to the horn. It was tricky work. Tristan dulled the blade with a whisper of spell, for safety.

Keep your fingers clear this time, Thomas advised.

The cat was right. The roots felt like the jaws of a trap. Tristan looked deep into the unicorn's eyes, trying to touch its mind. "You need to *push*," he told it. "Stop pulling back! *Push,* so I can spread the roots apart."

Did the horn under his hands glow more brightly? And if it did, did that mean anything? Tristan spoke a spell to stiffen the knife blade. Being only brass, it would never master the roots without magical help. Iron was stiff and kept a sharp edge—but cold iron was magic's enemy. It was deadly dangerous for a wizard to mess with. Even Blais left iron alone.

Tristan hoped his spell was strong enough. Once the knife began to bend, it was apt to go soft as butter in a heartbeat, an unfortunate backlash of the spell. The knife would be useless—and he had no other tool for attacking the roots.

Tristan wiped his palms dry. Wrapping his right hand around the knife's hilt, he rested his left hand on the crest of the unicorn's neck. Tangling his sore fingers in the long forelock, he pulled down, hard.

The head came forward, and so did the horn. Tristan felt the tension shift, where roots and horn and knife all met. The unicorn suddenly understood about pushing *into* the trap. It thrust forward with all its strength. Cloven hooves dug into the sand. The white back humped.

Tristan yanked his fist hard to the right. The knife levered at the roots. The roots spread, so slightly that the change could only be felt, not seen.

"Now!" Tristan shouted. He let loose of the forelock and pushed back hard on the unicorn's head. Sand flew as the silver body surged backward. The horn rasped free of the black roots, like a sword clearing a scabbard. Tristan rolled to one side, landing on his back. He still held his knife. Its blade curved hard sideways. Tristan decided he could mend it. If not with magic, then with a mallet and a flat stone. Whatever it took. Later, when he'd caught his breath.

The unicorn shifted into forward motion. It tore toward the edge of the ground, bounding over Tristan on the way.

Either Tristan's wards or the black water stopped it. The unicorn veered violently to its left, sending up sheets of sand. Thomas leapt out of its path. Tristan flattened himself against the dead tree.

Three times the unicorn circled the little hill of dry ground. It went to its left, then to its right, then back to the left. It halted. It threw back its head. The dim rusty circle of the moon rode just above the tip of its horn. It cried out sharply.

The unicorn sounded as desperate as it had looked before Tristan released it. He was amazed that his wards bound it to the hillock. How could his little spells affect a creature so full of magic?

Perhaps they did not. There were shapes out there, half invisible in the dark. They hovered over the dark water. Some of them must have had wings, by the drifting way they moved to and fro. While he watched them, Tristan's stomach twisted uneasily. He wasn't sure why—they were so dark and moved so quickly, they were never much more than shadows.

Shadows with *teeth*. One snapped at Thomas, sitting close by the water. The cat swatted reflexively at the shapes as they passed temptingly near. Fortunately, the wards seemed to be holding. The flash of teeth could be seen, but that was all.

"Don't break the circle!" Tristan warned the cat urgently.

I'm not a fool. The tip of Thomas' tail flicked impatiently.

"I don't think they can do more than tease us. But it's better if they don't get in," Tristan added nervously.

Thomas yawned, showing all *his* teeth. It might be a fair fight, if it came to that.

With a shuddering sigh, the unicorn sank to the ground. The proud head stayed up for a moment. It stared at the shadows.

Tristan watched it. It seemed willing to accept him, so long as he didn't approach it. Maybe it understood that his wards held the bog-haunts at bay. Maybe it was grateful. Certainly it was exhausted. It bent its neck and rested its muzzle upon one foreleg. The dark eyes closed.

Tristan felt his own eyelids drooping. He dragged them open. There were but one or two hours remaining till dawn, judging by the stars. All seemed well with the wards. Resting should be safe.

Tristan was so worn out, the sand under him felt almost soft. He wrapped his cloak around him. He lay down. The bog-haunts chittered angrily, but their voices soon faded. In a dozen heartbeats they were no more than the croaking of frogs, the whisper of the night wind through the reeds.

TURN ABOUT

When Tristan opened his eyes, the air was bright silver. He blinked. A dense mist had risen. He could see no farther in sunlight than he had in the darkness.

A pale circle overhead showed where the sun stood. Already it was too high to give Tristan a true bearing. Not that he could see a horizon anyway. He couldn't see *anything* more than a dozen paces away.

In daylight, the unicorn was the color of pearls. Damp had sprinkled a royal ransom of diamonds upon its mane. The long forelock draped lank on either side of the softly shining horn. Its white eyelashes were so long that they curled up at the tips.

Teardrop nostrils rounded, sniffing curiously at the crumbs of oatcake Tristan offered. Lips softer than silk velvet accepted his gift.

Thomas snorted at such a pathetic breakfast. Plaintively, he inquired as to whether he might break the wards and try his luck at fishing.

"We're going," Tristan told him. "The wards will break anyway. But maybe you should stay close. You don't want to get lost."

We're already lost. Any reason I should starve as well? And away Thomas stalked.

Chewing at the end of his first finger, Tristan watched a heron winging overhead with dreamlike slowness. Herons nested in trees. *Big* trees. Was the bird going *to* or *from* its rookery? Surely so early, it would be on its way to a favorite fishing spot.

If he could retrace the heron's course, that should bring him out of the bog. Once the sun burned the mist off, he'd be able to see farther. He would be glad of that. Having the world end for all appearances a dozen paces away was unsettling.

The unicorn watched as Tristan gathered up the bee skep. "You'd better come too," he told the creature. "You can't stay here." There seemed to be neither food nor clean water anywhere near. The liquid in the root-locked pool was inky black even under the sun.

Tristan took off his belt and buckled it around the unicorn's neck for a collar. His hank of fishing line made a fragile leash. Tristan tugged gently at it, whispering a spell to the linen cord. The unicorn splashed into the water after him, its steps absurdly high. It did not trust the bog.

The air warmed. Insects awoke. Tristan slapped at something biting his cheek. Not far off, a green-eyed fly droned. It went past, then circled back, plainly hoping for a meal. The dragonflies which would happily hunt such bloodsuckers were still prisoners to a chilly armor of dewdrops. Until the sun grew stronger, they could not take to the air. Tristan said his repelling incantation once more. It kept perhaps one insect in ten from discovering the unprotected parts of his skin.

Thomas bounced from tussock to reed-clump. Without warning, he bounded high into the air. Tristan suspected he had spotted a careless bird.

The cat landed out of sight, with a loud splash. He reappeared with a spotted frog in his jaws. The dangling legs kicked twice, then went still.

Want some? Thomas asked around his mouthful.

"No, thank you," Tristan answered faintly. His belly gave a kick rather like the dying frog's. Raw fish was a notion he might have considered. Raw frog was decidedly *not*. Tristan had no idea what the difference was, but it was very clear that there was one.

Suit yourself. Thomas crunched loudly, swallowed, and forged ahead once more. Looking for seconds.

Tristan tried not to imagine how a frog might taste. He concentrated on choosing a route through the bog. If he watched only his feet, he'd surely circle. That would have them back at the drowned tree within an hour. Yet if he *didn't* watch where he was going, he might stray into real trouble. Deep water was only inconvenient. Quicksand or bottomless mud would be deadly. He needed to keep a sharp eye out. It was difficult. The sunstruck mist was so bright, Tristan found he wanted to shut his eyes.

Underfoot, the mud seemed firmer. Tristan felt encouraged. Surely he was near some edge of the bog! A great excitement rose up in him, a singing that started in his heart and spread outward.

He was aware of the unicorn with every step. True, he had leashed it, but the line hung slack. The unicorn followed at his heels like a trained dog, of its own will. When Tristan halted, it rested its dainty muzzle upon his shoulder. It nibbled curiously at his hair, sniffed the backs of his ears, the nape of his neck. Its whiskers tickled his skin.

The affection astonished Tristan. It wasn't gratitude. Gratitude would have run off, the instant he'd freed the creature's horn from the tree. Instead, the unicorn had chosen to stay by him. Chosen *him*.

Tristan did not need his wizard's training to feel the magic within the unicorn. It gave off enchantment as the sun showered light and warmth, as flowers wafted out sweet scent. Now that he thought about it, the unicorn might be the reason his ward-spells had suddenly become so effective. Tristan had only said the insect-charm *once*. Nothing had bitten him afterward. That spell never worked so well. *Never*. He knew that unicorn's horn was powerful magic—how much stronger was a whole, living unicorn?

And this unicorn was *his*. Blais would not make him send it away. A unicorn was not a cat. A unicorn was an entirely different matter. And its magic would be the making of him as a wizard. Tristan could hardly breathe, just thinking of what might come to pass.

The mist burned away at last. Overhead, the sky was suddenly blue. The bogwater was still silver, but the grasses rising out of it and the moss and scum floating on it showed many shades of green. Thomas appeared, no longer hidden and certainly not camouflaged. The cat was soaked. He shook his fur, leaving it all spikes. He looked well-fed. He looked smug.

Tristan felt a pang. It wasn't Thomas' fault that he was what he was. So far he'd been the loyalest sort of companion in a difficult situation. No one could ask for a truer friend. Before Thomas, Tristan had never had a friend. It was wrong to send Thomas away, to swap the unicorn for the cat and think no more about it.

But…a *unicorn!* The most fleeting glimpse of one was a miracle. Most folk never saw one in a whole lifetime. The spell for summoning a unicorn in Blais' grimoire ran for twelve pages—and even so the results were not guaranteed. Yet here was *this* unicorn, close enough for Tristan to touch, touching *him* of its own accord. Tristan reached out to it. It seemed to enjoy the feel of his hands. He stroked along the line of the white jaw, then under it. Their cow *loved* to be scratched there.

Likewise the unicorn. It shut its almond eyes with pleasure. It tilted its head. It pressed against his fingers to encourage Tristan to continue. Tristan took the hint. His fingers ran over silk velvet, but warm and living. The bone beneath was a carving meant to be explored by touch. Every stroke invited another.

Just how big is this swamp, anyway? Thomas stood against Tristan's leg. His mouth was half open, as if he had just meowed for a saucer of cream.

Tristan blinked, trying to hear the question as it floated by him. He'd had little sleep. There was still mist inside his head, where the sun couldn't get at it. "I'm not sure," he answered at last. "It's on Blais' maps. I wasn't planning to come here. I didn't really look." Tristan frowned. "It varies with the rainfall, I suppose. And there's a river somewhere, I think." He felt more weary by the moment. If he could sit down, if he could shut his eyes for just one little minute...

So you're saying we're lost?

"We're *not* lost!" Tristan snapped. Why did the cat insist on pestering him? The unicorn didn't do that.

And we aren't walking in circles either?

Would a unicorn be less...argumentative? Tristan felt instantly ashamed of the thought. Also, he had a nagging suspicion that the cat might be right. He looked around deliberately, well beyond his next step.

By now, they really ought to have come out of the bog. They had not. There was pale sky overhead, half the world. The lower half was more varied. Mud, water, reeds and head-high grass waving in the wind. But no trees, and no dry ground.

Tristan's legs ached with walking. The notion of rest was a dream. He'd need to do it standing, for one thing. There was no even halfway dry spot anywhere in sight.

His stomach ached too. Tristan thought almost wistfully of Thomas' frog. Were the bog's waters deep enough for fish?

The sun stood directly over his head. It would drop in front of him, all through the long hours of the second half of the day. He could steer by that, Tristan decided. He began to walk once again. Standing still wasn't any use.

If he *had* circled, he might be retracing ground he'd already crossed. It should be the final time, at least. Once he'd come out onto solid earth, Tristan decided he would sit down for a bit. Make tea and porridge.

A low humming came from the bee skep. It felt like Thomas' purr, against his shoulder. After a bit, Tristan began to imagine that he could make sense of the buzzing, though he hadn't taken a taste of honey to help the spell along.

The bees were restless. They had cause for concern. Where was the proper home Tristan had promised them? Where were the many flowers? The bees felt the sun's heat upon their container, but they could not see the sun's bright face. They missed it. A day of rainy weather made bees cross. This long blind trek was worse still. They didn't like it.

Tristan thought of opening the linen sack. If he put a little honey in, the bees could feed. They might be hungry by now. Food would reassure them.

But a few bees were sure to slip past him, anxious and impatient, maybe confused. And they'd be lost, separated from their swarm and their queen. They'd die, unable to find either their old home or the new.

Or else they'd fly about questioning him. The mosquitoes were trial enough. Thanks to his spell, they weren't biting, but they hung about him in clouds. Tristan sneezed and thought he snorted out a couple of insects. Tiny gnats stunted about him too, and got in his eyes. Bees would be just too much to put up with.

The unicorn tossed its head. Tristan didn't see anything actually bite it, but the whine of wings near its ears plainly annoyed it. It gave the air a fierce slash or two with its horn, like a swordsman testing his weapon.

Trees, Thomas said. He was on Tristan's shoulder once more. Dry ground was scarcely even a memory.

Tristan lifted his head. He squinted. The sun had been in his eyes for the past hour. All he saw was a red glare. Blurry shapes might or might not be real objects.

Thomas stood tall. Then he scrambled to the top of Tristan's head, the highest vantage he could reach. Tristan was too startled to stop him. He just stumbled to a halt.

"What is it?" he asked, gritting his teeth.

Thomas turned about slowly, mindful of his balance. Better than digging his claws in, Tristan decided. And clever of the cat, taking advantage of his human height to check out all the directions. He ought to have sent Thomas up one of the drowned trees before, to see what could be seen. *"What?"* Tristan repeated impatiently.

You aren't going to like this, Thomas said. He sounded unhappy himself.

MOONSHINE

Deerlike hoofprints. The marks of boots. His *own* boots. Tristan understood what Thomas had guessed already. The bare trees were the very same drowned wrecks he'd put at his back that morning.

Tristan slumped to the soggy ground. He rested his head against his knees. He was well used to walking, but the recognition sucked the last strength from his legs.

At least he wasn't lost. Not anymore. Tristan opened his eyes and stared bleakly at the last red edge of the sun. Even without a map, he knew *exactly* where he was. Trouble was, he didn't know how to leave the place for more than a few hours.

Tristan's head buzzed with weariness. Or was that the bees? By now they must be cross indeed. Swarming bees might not sting, but Tristan was glad all the same for the thickness of the linen sack. His captives might soon choose to leave their prison of straw. The sack would prevent escapes…and arguments.

The sky shifted steadily from rose to lavender to deep blue. When the blue had become violet, the brightest of the stars showed themselves. If he took a bearing on one of them, Tristan thought he could try walking straight away from the hillock.

He could not muster will enough to climb to his feet, much less walk boldly. Tristan was worn out. His feet were soaked and swollen. His hips hurt. His knees ached. He was hours past being merely hungry. There was not an ounce of hope left in his heart, and all the stars looked alike to him. They'd be useless as guides. Tristan didn't care. He could not imagine that he would *ever* care.

A breeze circled about. It came, and it went, mysterious and unseen in the way of wind. But whenever it arrived, a faint chittering arrived with it. The sound was always *just* too faint for Tristan's ears to be sure of it. Frogs sang, loud, shrill, but this was something different. It seemed familiar. Tristan could not hold the thought. Like the wind, it teased and slipped away before he could grasp it.

Thomas placed a soft paw on his knee. *You'd better set the wards again,* the cat suggested. His eyes gleamed silver.

Tristan did not stir. If he heard, he gave no sign of it. His eyes were open, but empty as a sleepwalker's.

Are you dreaming? Thomas patted insistently at the knee. The cloth over it had been patched, more than once. *Weren't those things bad enough last night, when they couldn't actually get close?*

Tristan stared dully into the night. Thomas leaned into the boy's line of sight. No reaction. When he moved, Tristan's green eyes didn't follow him. Indeed, they scarcely blinked.

Thomas considered. He deliberately extended his claws. Needle-sharp tips pierced cloth, skin—and finally Tristan's shell of misery.

"Hey!" Tristan's eyes and mouth went wide.

Thomas gave him a bland look. *The wards?* the cat asked again.

Tristan scrubbed his face with his fingers. *The wards.* Yes. He ought to set the wards. It was important. He couldn't remember why, but it was. He got up clumsily. His eyes were sore. His head ached. His feet were huge and full of red-hot pins. Double-pointed pins.

You'll feel better with the wards in force, Thomas told him.

The cat paced alongside Tristan every step of the circuit around their bit of dry ground, including the twisty tree and the wide-eyed unicorn. Thomas made certain he laid the spells down exactly as he should. He was harder to satisfy than Blais ever had been, Tristan thought. He insisted that everything be done just so—as if he knew anything about it. He made Tristan repeat one difficult passage three times.

Lines of silver glowed on the ground. They wove a web in the air. The mark of the final hand-pass interlaced with the traces of the first, while Tristan spoke the final words. The air chimed like a crystal bell. Tristan rubbed his eyes again.

What's the matter? Thomas sniffed at the silver lines, which were slowly fading. There was no urgency in his manner now. He was entirely at ease.

"I feel strange. Like I'm dreaming and can't wake." Tristan shifted his fingers to the back of his neck. His head throbbed, but his thoughts came clearer, little by little.

The misty shapes were back. They flitted restlessly on the far side of the circle of wards. Tristan scowled at them, then turned his head away. He felt better if he didn't look.

He picked Thomas up and laid his cheek against the long soft fur. "I don't think I'd have set the wards in time, if you hadn't made me do it." He shivered, realizing how close the danger had been. Those things outside…wouldn't have *stayed* outside. "I don't think I'd have set them at all."

You wouldn't have, Thomas agreed, purring against his ear. *They didn't want you to.* He rubbed his head on Tristan's chin.

"Everything here is a trap. I forgot that."

You're welcome. The cat's head butted Tristan's jaw, softly. *Are you all right now?*

Tristan sighed. "I'm so *tired.* I'd fall asleep standing up, only I'm too hungry! And I have no reason to think I can get us out of here tomorrow—or in a month of tomorrows. But if you mean the bog-haunts, yes. They won't trick me again. And thank you," he added.

Don't mention it. I'm sure they'd be amusing to hunt, but I don't much want those things in here either. Whatever they are.

"Tricksters," Tristan said. He wouldn't give them more power than that. "Bog-haunts like to play pranks. Get you lost, lead you in circles. I don't really need *them* for that, do I?"

If you want to sleep, I'll stand guard.

Tristan searched the sky. "If the moon comes up bright, I could…there are paths you can only see by moonlight. Like the writing in Blais' books. I think I remember a spell that might help."

Something's wrong with the moon, Thomas said abruptly. *It's been dark too long.*

Lore claimed that the eyes of cats mirrored the moon's phases. Tristan knew that wasn't strictly true. But *was* there some affinity, all the same? Like to like? That was a fundamental principle of magic. What did Thomas know? What had he seen? Tristan felt a chill of foreboding. He couldn't chase the worry down to a logical cause, but he no longer felt sleepy.

The unicorn was watching the circling shapes too. When one came especially near, the creature tensed as if for flight. There was nowhere for it to run. If it crossed—and broke— the wards, it would be chased. Chased, and hunted till it died.

"Don't," Tristan advised softly. Maybe the unicorn had thought it was stabbing one of the tricksters, when it got its horn trapped. The bog-haunts would think that fine sport.

The unicorn tossed its head and looked at the sky. The shadows chattered, cheated of their victim—at least for that moment.

Thomas was right about the moon. Tristan discovered the tarnished circle of it in the sky—still low, but risen well clear of the horizon. It looked so odd without its shine. Incomplete. Unnatural.

There was no reason for the moon to be dark so long. Even when the old moon yielded to the slim crescent of the new, it merely vanished for a night or two. It didn't fade. None of Blais' books had ever said a word about a moon being veiled without dust or cloud or eclipse being involved.

Eclipse. Was that the answer? The moon looked as if it had never emerged from the eclipse's shadow. But Tristan had never heard of such a thing happening. To achieve it by means of a spell would require a very powerful magic indeed. Keeping the moon dark for so many nights was an awesome undertaking. What wizard had that kind of power? And what wizard would waste it so? What use was a dimmed moon?

It didn't consign the world to darkness. The bog wasn't especially dark without the moon. Particularly the magic-ringed area around the drowned trees. If Tristan hadn't chanced to spot the dim shape in the sky, he'd have assumed that all was perfectly well with the moon. The unicorn's silver hide shed a light that softly washed every nearby object. The horn was brighter still—almost too bright to look at without squinting.

Timidly, Tristan put out his hand. The unicorn did not flinch away from him. He ran his fingers down the crest of the long neck, from the ears to the shoulder. The unicorn's coat was soft and slippery as water—only warm, not cool. The feel of it invited another touch, and that touch another, and another. The unicorn appeared to enjoy the attention. A cat would have been purring. The unicorn made no sound, but it arched its neck beneath Tristan's fingers.

Without warning, it flung its head back. The tip of the horn traced an arc across the scattered stars. Tristan stepped back, startled. The unicorn's throat swelled. It gave a low cry. The sound came at Tristan through every inch of his skin, as well as his ears. It pierced the soles of his feet as he stood on them.

He didn't think he could listen to another such cry. He'd stop his ears with his fingers, or with mud. His heart would shatter if he heard that sound again. Fortunately, the proud head dipped after the single call. The unicorn turned its back upon the moon and upon the stars.

Tristan resumed stroking. Maybe he could gentle the sorrow out of it. He would reassure it, soothe it. The unicorn folded its slender legs and sank down. Tristan sat right beside it on the damp earth.

"I'll call you Moonshine," he said. "That's what you look as if you're made of. And once we're out of this bog, it won't be so bad. You'll like the meadows, and the orchard's always nice. Do you like apples? It's hard not to like apples." He leaned back against the silver shoulder. His eyelids drooped. Tristan dragged them up for a moment.

"I don't know whether Blais will let you sleep in the cottage. I don't know if you'll even want to. But it's nice in the winter. Sometimes the snow's halfway up the windows, but it's always warm, inside. Blais has spells to keep out the cold, and the old apple trees make the sweetest firewood. You can see pictures in the flames, and the smoke smells just like spring…"

Tristan drifted off into a tangle of memories. Moonlight shining on a silver field of snow. Moonbeams dancing over a sea of white apple blossoms, their billows like the sea's, only sweetly fragrant too. Unicorns smelled of flowers, Tristan realized. Maybe that was what they ate, blossoms. Like flowers, they made the air around them sweet. He breathed in the unicorn's scent, warm and cool both at once. Not quite a rose, nor yet a lily. Just a hint of cardamom...

Gentle as flowers. Yet unicorns were fearsome beasts too. Lions dared not stand against them. The merest paring from a unicorn's horn was an unfailing cure for any sort of poison and most sicknesses. A living unicorn was a thousand-fold more magical. And *this* unicorn belonged to *him*. Tristan could scarcely believe it—but here he was touching the unicorn, so the wonder must be true. He felt the unicorn sigh. He smelled violets and ripe apples and cinnamon.

What a wizard he could be, with a unicorn lending its magic to his own! There'd be no spell he could not master, no sorcery he could not command. His fame would spread far beyond little Dunehollow. Folk would journey for many leagues to buy spells and charms from him. Soon they'd be paying him with rubies and sapphires rather than shaved coins and salted fish. He could buy Blais a robe of red silk, Tristan decided. With stars and moons worked all over it in threads of gold, spangles of silver.

He wouldn't need chickens any longer. He and Blais could breakfast on peacock's eggs, if they chose. Actually, he wouldn't need the bees either. Tristan examined the idea sleepily. If he didn't need the bees, then he should let them go. For some reason, that was important.

Of course! The bees could guide him out of the bog. Water would not slow or baffle *them*. Bees owned the air. Bees flew away from their hives each day and easily returned. Bees were never lost.

If he let the bees go, he could follow them.

SWARM ON THE WING

The sun was an orange blotch on the misty edge of the world. All the world that could be seen, at least. Tristan undid the leather thong that secured the bag around the skep. Not a single bee emerged. The air was still cool. The bees were sleepy.

Tristan touched a drop of honey to the tip of his tongue. He poured the rest out in front of the skep. Then he waited.

In an hour, the sun had warmed the air and the bees awoke. One crawled over the lip of the sack, combing her fur with a leg while she walked on the other five. She brushed her antennae, like a drowsy boy rubbing his eyes. Tristan bespoke her. It was time, he said, for the swarm to send out its scouts.

Where flowerzzzzz? The bee asked at once, excited.

"Ahead," Tristan told her, feeling wretched. The swarm had believed his promises. "I'm sorry. I don't know any other way to get out of here."

No flowerzzzzz? The antennae flopped in confusion.

"Out there." Tristan gestured broadly with one hand. "Plenty of flowers. And if you want, I'll still take you with me, any that choose to come. But I can't get out of this bog. The last honey you ate won't last much longer. You must send the scouts out now, to find a new home."

Yezzzz. The bee combed a leg over her wings, her empty pollen baskets. *Scoutzzzzzz.* She hurried back into the sack.

The scouts soon appeared. The bees sipped honey and flew off, each taking a slightly different direction. Tristan made no attempt to track any of them. Right now, the bees were every bit as lost as he was. He must wait until a scout returned with news of a hive-site. When the entire swarm departed, he'd follow. The dark cloud of the flying swarm should be easy to keep track of. It was the best chance any of them had to get out of the bog.

Even swarming bees would not fly at night. That wasn't safe for the queen. The scouts must return no later than sun-high, in order to escort her to a new home. Anything farther away than that was too far. And just as well—Tristan would need light too, if he was to follow the bee-cloud. If it left too late in the day, he might find himself stranded in an even *worse* spot. If there was a lake out there, and if the bees flew across it—well, he couldn't do likewise. Nor could the unicorn.

Tristan watched the cloudless sky. His jaw was tense. His mouth was dry as dust—probably the only completely dry thing for leagues around. Thomas sat beside him, feigning nonchalance. The twitching tip of the cat's tail gave his true mood away.

The skep hummed, constant and low. The bees were impatient also.

Suddenly the humming increased in pitch till it became a purr. Tristan turned his head quickly. A bee was perched on the sack. Headfirst, she entered. Tristan got to his feet. He picked up the unicorn's tether.

The sack buzzed. It rumbled. The bees inside were highly agitated. But not a one left the skep. The scout's report must somehow have been lacking.

Other scouts winged in. One, then two. Half a dozen all at once. The skep rocked, as thousands of wings rustled within it. There was a heartbeat of absolute silence. Then, a roar.

Bees poured from the sack like smoke. They rose into the air. On and on they came, one tiny body after another. Hundreds, then thousands of them. The swarm cloud danced in the air, clustering about the queen. Marching order attained, it moved off with obvious purpose and no time wasted.

Tristan scrambled to follow. He snatched up Thomas with one hand and tugged at the unicorn's tether with the other. The empty skep was left where it sat. He splashed quickly down into the bog, slashing a way through the ward-circle as he went.

The unicorn hung back, reluctant to abandon the spot where it had twice been safe. Tristan pulled urgently at the cord. Already the swarm was distant. It looked little bigger than the palm of his hand. If it got to be a smaller speck than that, he'd lose sight of it, easily. He pulled. The linen thread snapped. The unicorn moved not a single step.

"I'm not leaving you!" Tristan shouted at it. "This is your chance to get out of here! Don't you understand? You have to trust me. The bees can lead us out."

He didn't really blame the unicorn for objecting. How was this any different from the day before, when they'd walked through mud and water and biting insects—and in the end been back just where they'd started? But if he couldn't make the beast move, they had *no* chance.

Quickly, Tristan unwound the skep's straw coil. A last sleepy bee flew out, buzzing. Tristan's fingers sketched a spell of binding over the coil. The magic would hold whatever he put the straw rope around—if it worked.

No time to doubt himself. Tristan dropped the rope over the unicorn's head. It settled about the base of the unicorn's neck, like a collar of pale gold. Tristan tugged. The rope tightened, the smallest bit. The unicorn took a startled step forward. The spell he'd used was a Binding, with more than a hint of a Compulsion worked in as well. Tristan's instincts had been sure. The unicorn was his to command. Quickly, he searched the sky for the cloud of bees. The unicorn took one stiff step after another, following him.

The swarm was alarmingly distant. It was almost impossible to find against the sky. Had there been other clouds, Tristan thought he could not have done it. But the sky was empty, and he spied the bees at last. Tristan set off. The unicorn walked without protest at his heels.

Water, mud, reeds all around. Endless empty sky above. For Tristan, the day was too much a copy of the one before. It felt like a nightmare. He wanted to wake, home in his own bed. He could not, of course.

The smudge of the swarm moved just at the edge of his sight. Tristan followed the bees, on and on. He splashed, he stumbled. He sought the driest ground, avoided the worst muck, held the straightest course he could. Always, he kept his eyes on the swarm-cloud.

At last he could no longer make it out. The sun sank red at his back. The sky ahead was dim and bleak. Darkness was coming on. But Tristan's tired feet were trying to tell him something important. The ground beneath his soggy boots had changed—it was firmer. Tristan took more false turns among half-seen tussocks of marsh grass. Suddenly he noticed a dim, dark mass ahead of him. *Trees.* The forest! Well, *some* forest. They were out of the bog.

There was no sign of the swarm. Tristan hoped the bees had reached safety. The trees would grant them refuge for the night. If need be they could hang in a damp clump from a branch, their bodies making living walls. Come dawn, they'd claim their new home, in whatever place their scouts had found for it.

Tristan wished them many flowers and all the nectar they could gather. They'd been more than patient. He felt he'd let them down, unable to take them to the haven he'd described so glowingly.

Now the stars overhead could be of some use to him. Tristan considered them and set off through the trees. He wasn't sure of his *exact* location, but in a general way he no longer felt lost. He was within a day's walk of the cottage— at worst two days' walk. Perhaps three. The important thing was, he could step wherever he wished. He might bump into a tree, but he wouldn't drown unless he fell into a river.

Tristan kept on through the wood so long as he could put one foot ahead of the other. Thomas bounded before him, delightedly stalking mice. Evidently frogs were boring prey, for all their high-jumping.

The unicorn followed at the end of the straw rope, its head drooping low. It must be exhausted, Tristan thought. It had lost its grace. Its pewter muzzle nearly dragged the leafy ground. Its silver hooves stumbled over roots.

Once relief at being out of the bog wore off, Tristan was faltering too. Perhaps they ought to rest. At least till the moon climbed high. It was too easy to trip in the dark, or fail to spot a low-growing branch not quite far enough overhead.

Tristan halted. The unicorn stopped. It simply stood. It did not sniff the air. It did not look about. Tired enough to sleep standing up, Tristan guessed with sympathy.

He looked around. A drift of soft leaves was what he wanted to see. That would make a softer bed than dry earth. Finding a good spot, he led the unicorn gently to it. The spell he'd used to make the rope still seemed enough to secure it. It went where he did, stopped when he stopped.

Tristan smiled in the dark. His spells *were* stronger, since he'd found the unicorn. Its magic *was* helping his own. When they had been friends for more than a handful of days, who knew what might happen? What might they not do? He settled for sleep.

Tristan's dreams were pleasant. Contentment swelled his heart. The leaves were soft under him, and the unicorn was warm beside him. His dreams were full of the creature.

No one was going to laugh at him now. No one would pity him. He'd have respect. He'd be a proper wizard at last. All the things Blais had struggled to teach him would bear fruit, beyond his wildest hopes. The world was his. He held it in his hand. It was warm against his back. Tristan had never known such happiness, such excitement, such wonderful peace.

THE PRISONER

Tristan sat up, blinking. For a moment, he had no idea where he was. *Who* he was felt entirely out of reach.

He was cold. Something was wrong, but Tristan could not, half asleep, decide just what. He groped after the last shreds of his dream, but awake he couldn't hold them. The loss tasted bitter, like drinking seawater.

Oh. The unicorn was on its feet. That must be what had disturbed him. It pulled gently at the rope, testing the binding of straw and spell. Tristan had looped the rope about his left wrist while he slept. Held, the unicorn stopped where it was. It did not struggle. It stood still, a statue of silver.

Overhead, the moon had risen. It was still dim, tarnished. Tristan was used to that now. He could make it out, centered in a gap between leafy branches.

The unicorn was looking at the moon too. It pulled once more at the rope.

Did it think they should move on? Tristan had intended to, but the dim moon gave scarcely any light. Tristan felt he would rather wait for the sun. His brief sleep had showed him just how weary he was. It couldn't be long till dawn, and it would be so much easier to move through the wood in daylight, when he was rested.

The unicorn itself gave off light. It wasn't merely reflecting the starlight that fell upon it. Hide and horn shone bright enough to show him Thomas, sitting among the gnarled roots of a beech tree a dozen feet away. The cat's eyes shone silver-green, but their expression wasn't one Tristan could read at a distance.

Again the unicorn tipped its slender head toward the sky. The fluted horn seemed almost to touch the moon. That was an illusion, of course. A trick of sleep-sanded eyes. The moon was far, far out of reach. Only children believed they could actually *touch* the moon when it hung full in the sky.

Was it too weary to rest? Tristan could recall once or twice being too exhausted to sleep. Blais had dosed him with catnip tea and warm milk. What would soothe a unicorn? He had no milk, but he *did* have a few leaves of catnip. He could make a fire, now that there was dry fuel. He could make tea.

Tristan rose. He went hand over hand along the rope till he reached the unicorn's shoulder. Maybe a friend's touch would calm the creature. The unicorn turned its head, and Tristan's fingers brushed across the spiral horn.

Images flooded through his head, like water dumped carelessly into a bowl. They rushed past, no more than jumbled fragments which seemed to catch behind his eyelids.

Tristan saw the fat full moon sliding into the deep velvet of the eclipse. He watched the silver moonshine slip free of the moon. Drawn to the glitter of water far below, it dove through the dark air. It took shape as it went—the shining beams mingled and jelled. They became a silver beast with a single, shining horn. The unicorn had swift, slender legs, a long neck, a proud head. For part of one night, then moonshine was free. Free to dance. Free to roam.

But the earth below was sucking mud and faithless quicksand. The gleaming water was nothing less than a trap. The flitting, chittering dwellers of the bogland had laid their snare with all the cunning they could muster. The unicorn was deceived. It was tangled in a maze of shadows, of mud. It was tricked by the mirror of the water. And as it sought to flee, its precious horn was seized. Its mane was snared by the black branches of a dead tree's bones, wrapped round and round.

Wind whipped it, teased it with the hope of freedom. Darting shapes tormented it. However it moved, it was caught, held closer and closer yet. Soon, it was snared so completely that it could scarcely stir a cloven hoof.

Small wonder that the moon remained dark when the eclipse ended. Without her shine, the moon's face would always be a mere shadow upon the sky. The unicorn must go back. It must return home, or never again would the moon paint the earth with silver. Never would she wash the land with pearl.

But the unicorn was a prisoner still, more bound than ever.

Tristan tightened his grip on the rope. He took his hand from the horn and shook his head as if to chase a dream away. Let his unicorn go? No! That would never do. The unicorn was *his*. He'd found it. He'd saved it. He'd led it out of the bog, dragged it behind him every step.

The unicorn's head drooped, as if it had received his thoughts along the straw rope. Its eyes closed, long lashes hiding the dark almonds.

"No," Tristan told it, his voice harsh. He stroked the unicorn's neck. Its hair was like warm silk. "I can't," he said more gently.

You can't? Or you won't? Thomas asked. He still sat among the roots. *Has it changed one prison for another, then?*

"What do you know about it?" Tristan snapped, sharper than he meant. "You're just a *cat!"*

Thomas blinked at him. The cat said nothing more. He raised a paw and washed it. Tiny, precise strokes of his tongue adjusted every hair till each lay in place. He didn't look at Tristan again. His contempt could not have been made more clear.

Tristan turned his back on the cat. Thomas didn't understand, that was the thing. He *was* only a cat, after all. Not an apprentice who longed so desperately to be a wizard. Not an apprentice who'd studied and practiced and still found his desire to be as elusive as…as moonshine! Thomas didn't understand what his meddling had touched.

Since he'd found the unicorn, Tristan's spells had force. They had real power. They did what he meant them to do. Sometimes they did better. The hasty enchantment he'd thrown upon the straw rope—it was still holding just fine!

None of his most painstakingly crafted incantations had ever been half so effective. Even when his spells had more or less worked, it had never been like *this*. Tristan understood for the first time how *power* felt, what it was like to *know* that his spells would make magic and not just a mess.

If he let the unicorn go, he gave up all that. This wasn't like snatching a bird from a cat's paws and helping it return to the sky. If he let the unicorn loose, he would lose its magic. And his own magic without it was so…unreliable.

Without the unicorn, he'd be as he was before. He would have *nothing*. No hopes. No dreams. No glow of power to warm him.

He'd be the wizard's brat again, that's all he'd be. Blais' apprentice, that couldn't clean ashes out of the fireplace. Blais' apprentice because the wizard knew he had nowhere else to go!

Tristan wrapped the rope around his hand, three times. That used up all the slack, and it couldn't come undone by accident, either. He'd build the unicorn a stable, once he got it home. Not a lean-to like the one that sheltered the cow at night. No, a proper stable. He'd be able to do that. Why, he could make the logs saw *themselves* into boards!

He'd bed the stall with the most tender hay, with the long leaves and yellow flowers of sweet flag. He'd use flowers of every sort. And a bucket of silver, for drinking water. All the best. That was what the unicorn would have. It would not suffer for staying with him.

Tristan looked at the unicorn fiercely, as if he could hold it with his eyes alone. Once the moon had set, it would forget all this nonsense. He'd have it home before the moon rose again. In the stable, it wouldn't be able to *see* the moon. It wouldn't be troubled.

It was his. He'd keep it safe.

The unicorn began to weep. It didn't make a sound, but tears of crystal caught the starlight. The almond eyes looked ancient as the sky. Empty of stars, they were all darkness. Save for the flowing tears, they could have been the eye-holes of a mask.

The longer he looked at those eyes, the worse Tristan felt. He turned his head away. He tried hard to think about his future. Perhaps he'd be a greater wizard than Blais. That was how wizardry worked. Every wizard built on what those who'd gone before him had learned, what they had recorded in their grimoires, what they had written in their treatises on the Arts Magical. Tristan had known despair, certain he would never be a part of that tradition. But he *could.* He knew it now. All his work, all his study, would be rewarded at last.

Its muzzle was impossibly soft, as if a silk-tree had been crossbred with a peach. Surely unicorns must feed on only the tenderest of flowers. Well, it would have them! Whatever it needed. Flowers, rare fruits. Dew to drink, if that was what it preferred.

The unicorn's neck arched like a swan's. There its flesh felt different, for the silken skin stretched over muscle, not just sculptured bone. Tristan scratched timidly along the roots of the white mane, having heard that horses enjoyed that attention. All he knew of large animals concerned cows—specifically, their elderly milk-cow. She was a touch eccentric, after years of exposure to Blais and his magic. She might not any longer even be typical of cows. She liked to have the base of her tail scratched, and the space between her jaws rubbed.

The unicorn gave no sign that it enjoyed his scratching, but neither did it draw away from Tristan's fingers. When he reached its shoulder, the mane dwindled. A line of longer hair ran along the unicorn's spine, until it met and joined with the tail. Perhaps a unicorn could raise that crest of hair at will, the way cats did. It was written that unicorns were fierce fighters. They killed lions without trouble and did not hesitate to match their strength against dragons.

The legs were like a deer's, very slender. Longer than a cow's. Nothing to them but bone and sinew. The cloven hooves glistened like the pearly insides of oyster shells. Their tips were sharp as knives. That was how unicorns killed lions.

The shining horn was an endless spiral. He didn't want to risk touching it again, but Tristan could imagine no harm in *looking* at it. The tiniest shaving from it would ransom a king, and it could preserve that king from any poison. Almost no one ever saw a whole unicorn's horn. Fewer still saw it attached to the living unicorn. Tristan's heart ached with the wonder of that. He hoped he would never grow so used to the sight that he went numb to it. He didn't want to be blind and deaf to such a wonder. He swore he would not. He pledged it fiercely in his heart.

The straw rope was coarse. Its fibers were prickly as thistles. Tristan slid his fingers beneath the collar, scratching and soothing. The unicorn rested its chin upon his shoulder. It sighed deeply.

Good. It was settling. He'd known it would. It would sleep. Then he could do likewise. The moon would set. The sun would rise. He would lead the unicorn through the forest and back to Blais' cottage. There, he'd begin to discover what it was like to *truly* be a wizard.

Tristan's heart was full, but his stomach hurt. He couldn't have eaten anything that disagreed with him—the little food he'd carried was long gone. He'd actually eaten nothing in the past day but those few drops of honey while he spoke with the bees.

Most likely, his belly hurt because it was *empty.* That made sense. He could endure hunger for a few hours more. No trouble there. Still, Tristan felt odd. Sleep would not come.

The shadowy moon overhead caught his eye, and his stomach twisted, hard. Tristan looked away—straight at the unicorn.

It was staring at the moon again. No tears fell from its long eyes now. Nor did it cry out. No shrieks, no groans. It only watched, as the moon drew slowly across the sky.

Tristan felt another twinge, this one right under his heart. He swallowed hard, shoving the pain away. He'd had plenty of practice with that sort of thing. It *hurt* to watch his spells fail, no matter the care he took with them. It hurt to be friendless, to want a friend so much that he'd take any chance to gain one—let Rho sport with him, let Jock trick him and trap him and torment him.

His whole *life* hurt, most days. Tristan knew pain, even if he had no idea who he truly was or why his parents had abandoned him. They'd left a helpless baby in an orchard one winter's night. Had they known Blais would find him? Had they cared? Was he truly an orphan—or merely discarded? He didn't know. He doubted he ever would know.

Pain was constant. Tristan was used to it. The unicorn was not, yet, but it was learning. It looked once more at the moon. Then it lowered its head, so that the tip of its horn nearly dragged the ground.

Something in the gesture alarmed Tristan. What if it could *die* of pain, of despair? He had rather often wished that *he* could. What if it died *right now,* as the last of its hope left it? Tristan knelt and flung his arms around the unicorn's head. It seemed heavy as a coffin. Dead weight.

Don't, he wished it urgently. *Stay with me. Please!*

A warm drop slid onto his cheek, where it pressed against the unicorn. Tristan's throat felt swollen, hot. It began to ache.

Again, his fingers touched the rope of straw. They slid beneath it, against the slippery silken hair. Tristan wrenched them back, so fast that the rope burned his skin.

No! I can't. I can't!

Can't you?

He couldn't if he thought about what he was doing. If he counted what he was losing. Tristan acted swiftly, before he could sort out consequences. Sketching a Dismissal with the fingers of his left hand, he gave a mighty yank upon the straw rope with his right.

The tough fibers parted like cobwebs, once the magic left them. The unicorn leapt up and over Tristan, like a wave breaking over a stony shore. Unlike a wave, it never fell back. It rose upward and upward, into the sky.

Tristan jumped up too, snatching after the silver shape, after his dreams. He couldn't help himself. He grabbed at the unicorn, but his fingers captured only empty air. He lost his balance, stumbled and sprawled helplessly. The earth smacked him, solid as only the real world could be.

HOME AT LAST

Clouds swept over, on a cold wind whistling between the treetops. For a moment the wood went very dark. Tristan lay on his back. His eyes were wide open, staring at nothing. There seemed no point in his getting up. He only breathed because his lungs were in the habit and insisted on working whether he paid attention to them or not.

The clouds parted again. A waning moon shone down, thin as a reaper's sickle, but bright as it should be. In the shining curve of it, Tristan could plainly see the shape of the unicorn. It was home safe at last. Tristan's stomach stopped hurting him, though he hardly felt better. His heart was like a block of wood in his chest.

Thomas patted a velvet paw on his cheek. *You all right?*

Tristan rolled to one side. He sat up. He brushed leaves out of his hair. "I forgot you were here."

He didn't answer Thomas' question. Thomas could see he wasn't hurt. But all right? He might never be that again, Tristan felt. Never.

* * * *

Tristan slept the rest of the night, a rest heavy as stone, barren of dreams. When he woke, he was still tired to his bones. The air was silver with mist again. The trunks of the trees were gray—dark and light, but always gray. All color, all life, had vanished. They'd left the world when the unicorn jumped back to the moon.

Tristan was soaked with the mist, except for a little spot on his left side. Thomas was curled there. The cat's fur was covered with drops of water. Tristan ran a finger over the hair, and Thomas jumped up, hissing. He stalked away, tail fat as a bottle-brush.

In the mist, all directions looked just alike. To Tristan's heart they *were* alike, except for the way which led to the bog. He put that at his back and began walking. When the sun rose, the mist turned to gold, but his spirits stayed gray.

The wood was a confusing place. Half-hidden, thick with shadowy tree trunks and lanced by spear-shafts of bright light. To keep from circling back toward the bog, Tristan walked with the light straight in his eyes. He couldn't see much of where he was going. Once, he started sneezing and walked straight into a tree.

Thomas popped up at his side. *I found strawberries,* he announced.

That meant breakfast—and either a clearing or the edge of the forest. Tristan followed the cat and gathered the small red berries. Thomas crunched something with great zest, but Tristan made it a point not to find out just what it was. The berries tasted sweet.

The mist lifted until it became blue sky. The color was deep enough to break a heart—if that heart was not cracked already. Tristan looked about and decided that he knew where he was. He and Blais had come this way one spring, seeking mushrooms. If he was right, he would need to walk all day to get home, and most of the night too.

And just as well. He was going home without the unicorn and its magic, without the bees to trade for a laying hen. Not to mention *with* the cat he'd been ordered to get rid of. The longer his journey took, the better, Tristan felt.

He ate all the berries he could find, but when the first bees started visiting the grassland, Tristan abruptly set off. The furry insects reminded him that he'd failed even the bees. He hadn't taken them to the home he'd promised them. They had surely found *some* dwelling place, but it wouldn't be the paradise of flowers he'd put into their hearts. He'd have no hen, and Mistress Dalzell would have no honey. All his fault, every bit of it. No question about any of it.

Failure nagged like a pebble in his boot as Tristan walked. It was impossible to ignore the truth of it. There was a greater stone where his stomach ought to have been. The berries lay uneasily around it. As the day warmed, sweat made his clusters of insect bites itch like fire. Tristan frowned with displeasure at his shadow. It was a spindly thing, of no account, and it would not leave off trailing after him.

His shadow shrank to a puddle under his boots. Persistent, it reappeared in front of him and grew again. It stretched impossibly before it faded into the twilight, but it was never the shadow of a great wizard. It never would be. It was only the shadow of an apprentice who kept growing out of his patched clothes. A pity he could not likewise grow into his master's teachings, Tristan thought gloomily.

Eventually the moon lit his way. Tristan flinched from the silver light. He wished for clouds with all his heart. Finally he crept into the darkness under a holly bush and dozed fitfully until the moon set. That meant he had to walk in the dark, but Tristan didn't care.

* * * *

He arrived home with the sun. Blue smoke was curling out of the cottage chimney. Blais was home.

Tristan hardly cared. After all his other failures, his inability to slip back home unnoticed did not much surprise him. He ought to have expected Blais to come back early from Master Sedwick's.

As Tristan was crossing the yard, the cottage door opened. His master came out through it. Blais was carrying his scrying bowl.

Tristan didn't see what his master held, any more than he noticed Blais' relieved expression. He wasn't looking for either. Tristan kept his attention on the scuffed toes of his boots. They weren't dry yet.

"I have to tell you about the chickens," he began, to have it out and not look as if he was avoiding the disaster. "There was an eclipse of the moon, and I forgot to adjust the wards for it. A fox got in while I was at the shore gathering stones on the tideline."

"Yes, I saw the coop," Blais said mildly.

Tristan had cleaned the coop. But of course the bloodstains had soaked into the wood, and they would be perfectly visible—especially to a curious wizard trying to discover where his chickens and his apprentice had gotten to.

Blais set the scrying bowl down on the bench beside the door. "I thought you'd gone away for good, boy."

"Mistress Dalzell said she would give me a laying hen if I could bring her a swarm of bees. I thought I'd be back before you got home, sir."

Blais sighed. He scratched the back of his neck.

Tristan supposed it must be obvious that he had no hen with him, nor any bees either. He wondered whether Blais had been about to use the scrying bowl to locate him—or whether he'd *already* used it. Tristan forged ahead with his confession.

"I found wild bees that were ready to swarm," he said. "But I had to let them go. I couldn't get out of the bog except by following the swarm."

"The bogland is dangerous country." Blais frowned, his expression going distant. "You were fortunate to escape it."

Stupid to go into it, his master probably meant. Blais was just too polite to say so. "I know," Tristan admitted. "Even the moon got trapped there." He told Blais about the unicorn. How he'd seen it shining, how he'd released it and led it out of the bog—and how he'd let it go.

He heard Blais sigh again. He wouldn't be told he'd been dreaming, Tristan thought. He wouldn't be beaten for telling lies. There were advantages to being apprenticed to a wizard rather than the butcher. Not many, true—but nothing was so strange that Blais would doubt his account of it.

"You did the right thing, Tristan," his master said. "I would miss the moon, and not only for the spell-books I could no longer read. You did right."

"When I touched the unicorn, my spells *worked,*" Tristan said bitterly.

"And they will work again." Blais put an arm around Tristan's shoulders and squeezed once. "Your magic must grow, as your body has. You're growing yet—though I do hope that stops while you can still get through the doorways. Stooping is bad for the back." He sat down on the bench and held the bowl in his lap.

Tristan's expression refused to lighten. Blais tried again. "You certainly won't remember it, but you couldn't walk, the first time you tried," the wizard said. "You could *stand*—but one single step and down you went! And then you yelled, loud enough to wake the dead! You kept at it. Presently, you learned. You learned so well that you don't think about walking at all, now. You just *walk*, when you choose to." Blais nodded to himself. "Your magic will be like that. It may seem longer coming, but you're older now. You notice time passing. You grow impatient. Now come here, apprentice. There's something I need to show you." Blais arose from the bench, scooping up the bowl.

As they entered the cottage, Tristan heard birdsong. He stopped. He stared at a wicker cage hanging beside the window. Inside it, a blue and white canary was singing, his throat swelling like a frog's. The bird's whole body shook with melody. Finally the canary could not keep even so still—he bounced from one perch to another, trilling all the while. He repeated one piercing note three times, fell silent for a moment, then hopped close to the wicker bars. He cocked his dark-capped head toward Tristan and chirped inquiringly.

"Who's this?" Tristan asked in just the same tone.

"Ah. That is Minstrel," Blais said. "A gift from Master Sedwick. No new potatoes this time, I fear, but his song-birds have been efficient parents. They hatched out six chicks and have nested again."

"He's ours?" Tristan leaned closer to the cage, put one finger out. Minstrel hopped from perch to perch, scattering seed husks and a tiny feather or two. He eyed the finger.

Thomas had trailed Tristan through the cottage door. The cat's attention was fixed on the songbird—eyes, ears, quivering whiskers. Tristan tried to shove the cat back out the door with a look. He wasn't quite willing to use his boot, however gently. Thomas ignored him, sat, and licked the tip of his nose thoughtfully.

"You'll find his cage easier to clean than the chicken coop, but I'll want it done more often," Blais said. "And he wasn't what I wanted you to see, Tristan."

Tristan obediently turned his back on the birdcage. Blais was drawing himself up very straight, as if angry about something. Though what misdeed might actually be *worse* than letting the chickens be massacred, Tristan could not imagine. Well, he'd obviously failed to get rid of the cat—but was that so horrible? It wasn't as if he couldn't still take Thomas to Dunehollow. He braced for whatever was coming, trying not to be obvious about it.

"Tristan, one of your duties is to keep this house clean," Blais began climbing the ladder, beckoning Tristan to follow. "Now, I know that this is *your* bed, but it is in *my* house." Blais waved an arm, making his sleeve flap. "When was the last time you aired these blankets—or even straightened them?"

Blankets?

His master forgave him the dead chickens and fussed over unaired blankets? Tristan frowned and tried to answer the question. It was difficult—he hadn't been near the cottage, much less his bed, for the past several days. So much had happened. The night of the eclipse, he'd scarcely slept at all, and before that there'd been a string of hot, close nights. The loft had been airless. He'd slept in the orchard, studying constellations until his eyelids were too heavy to keep open.

"It's certainly a month," Blais reckoned sternly.

Tristan supposed it might be, one way and another. And Blais was right—the blankets ought to be aired. One had to go all winter without being able to do that properly, but in summer bedding could be spread on the clean grass, in the sun. Sunlight was a great freshener.

Still, he'd have expected his master to show more concern over his *own* bed. *It's not as if I have fleas,* Tristan thought, feeling misjudged. Mostly, though, he was just confused.

"You know, it takes a hen three weeks to hatch out her eggs," Blais said. "And most of a week to lay a nestful in the first place. Obviously, this one felt her eggs were less apt to be disturbed in your unmade bed than in the henhouse. As it happens, she was correct."

Tristan looked past Blais, into the narrow, slant-ceilinged loft. There, in a tangle of bedding, sat their red hen. Her yellow eyes glowered.

She looked odd. What was she sitting *on*, besides the heap of blankets? All at once, Tristan noticed a bit of eggshell, and some dark fluff under the hen shifted. A tiny head poked out from the red feathers. A tinier beak opened. The chick cheeped softly. A brother or a sister answered it, further beneath the hen's sheltering wings.

Chicks! They had their flock back again, in miniature and in time! Hens and surely a rooster or two as well—

Blais' shoulders were shaking. He was, Tristan realized, *laughing*.

"She must have grown weary of losing her eggs to you, day after day," the wizard chuckled. "So she made a hidden nest. In the last place she felt you'd look. I fear she's a most contemptuous bird."

"No," Tristan contradicted exuberantly. "I love her! She's the finest hen in all Calandra! If she's smarter than I am, I don't mind a bit! I wouldn't care if she laid cockatrice eggs!"

Blais pursed his lips. "I don't know if I'd go quite *that* far. But as you see, our lack of hens is remedied, or will be. These little one won't lay for months yet, but the red hen will still give us the odd egg or two—assuming you can outwit her and get hold of them."

The red hen rose to her feet, shaking her feathers to settle them. She clucked to her chicks, and they tumbled into raggedy line behind her. Tristan had to carry the chicks down the ladder, but then the little parade marched across the cottage and out into the yard.

SOMETHING ABOUT A HERO

"I'm afraid the cat still must go."

Tristan glanced automatically at Thomas. The cat sat frozen and fascinated beneath the canary cage. Minstrel appeared unconcerned—but the canary was young and inexperienced. He didn't know danger when he saw it. He thought his cage kept him safe. "I know," Tristan agreed in a low voice.

"I'm sorry, Tristan." Blais sounded as if he truly *was* sorry.

"Thomas went with me, you know. As if we were two heroes on a quest. I didn't know a cat would do that."

Blais looked away. He rubbed at the bridge of his nose, always a sign that he didn't wish to answer a question. Even a question that wasn't asked.

"And I think he kept me out of trouble, a time or two," Tristan went on. "He reminded me about setting wards—he made me set them, so the bog-haunts couldn't play tricks on me. I didn't want to. I was tired. I suppose the bog-haunts were already touching me, but I didn't know it. Thomas scratched me till he got my attention."

"Tristan." Blais rubbed his nose again.

"I know." He hadn't intended to stall, or beg. He was just reporting what he remembered. He hadn't paid it enough heed, at the time. "Thomas, go outside."

After one wistful glance at the birdcage, Thomas got up and went.

"Master Sedwick trains his birds to carry messages," Blais said. "They sing, of course, but they're quite intelligent and very responsive. I thought you'd enjoy having Minstrel here."

"Oh, I will." Tristan put a finger into the cage, between the wicker bars. Minstrel hopped close, cocking his head to one side, then the other, till he'd had a good look. He gave Tristan's finger a quick nibble, nothing at all like a hen's sharp pecks. Tristan saw his tiny tongue, dark red and sword-pointed. He felt it flick his finger before Minstrel hopped back away. Tristan supposed a bird might like to be stroked, much as a cat did. He could find out.

"I do like him," he assured Blais. "And I know it isn't fair to keep a cat in here with him. I'll walk Thomas back to Dunehollow before dark. I'll make him understand he has to stay there."

"Perhaps Mistress Dalzell would like a cat," Blais suggested.

"She wanted honey," Tristan said.

"You may take her some," Blais told him. "'Twould be only neighborly. And our bees will swarm one day, next year if not this. If Mistress Dalzell still needs bees, she may have them."

"I'll tell her when I bring the cow home."

"Ah!" Blais looked relieved. "*That's* where the cow is. I didn't think a fox could take a cow, but the cow was not here, and the fence was still whole."

"I didn't want to leave her with no one to do the milking," Tristan explained. "I never *did* get any butter churned." He hung his head as he realized that. Looking down, he noticed chicken scratches in the dirt.

He'd just sent Thomas outside. The hen and her train of chicks were in the yard, scratching for bugs. New-hatched chicks were probably *much* easier to catch than frogs.

Tristan went out the door very quickly.

The dooryard was quiet, empty. No sign of the red hen. Not so much as a feather. No sign of Thomas, either.

Tristan went round the cottage, heading for the henhouse. He hadn't taken three steps before he heard flapping and furious squawking. Tristan broke into a sprint, his heart pounding.

Chicks ran in all directions, scattering at their mother's urgent command. A streak of rust-red flashed out from beneath the henhouse. Jaws snapped at a pale yellow chick.

The fox! Its den must be *under* the coop! And now its luncheon had strolled right up to its waiting mouth. Tristan yelled, but even if he'd had a spell ready to throw, he couldn't be fast enough. And his hands were empty, useless. The chick was doomed!

Then Thomas sprang. He'd waited unseen in the shadow of the coop. The cat landed smack on the fox's red back. He latched on with every claw. He yowled like something that would be right at home in any haunted bog.

The startled fox sprang straight up into the air. It snapped its narrow jaws back over its shoulder, but Thomas was just out of reach. Safe himself, he could easily nip at the fox's pointed ears—and he did.

Tristan snatched up the wooden pitchfork and ran to help. The hen led her children to safety, under cover of the confusion. Footsteps slapped as Blais came running.

A little help here! Thomas suggested. *Just don't let him go back under there when I jump clear. Keep him running!*

"He came from under the coop!" Tristan shouted to Blais, as his master arrived.

The wizard understood. Stooping, Blais found a pebble. He flung it into the shadow beneath the coop. As it rolled into the fox's tunnel, Blais gestured sharply, shouting a word of command.

The single pebble instantly became a thousand. The fox's den was packed full of gravel in a heartbeat. The fox spun into the entrance as it finally shook Thomas loose. The stones clogging the den turned it back. Deflected, it met Thomas once more. The cat's back was arched. His every hair stood on end. Thomas' mouth was open wide, displaying his weaponry.

The fox swerved hard, then raced for open country and his life. Tristan ran a few yards after him, just to be sure the clever beast kept going and tried no further tricks.

When he returned, Blais was still standing in the yard. A frown creased the wizard's forehead, narrowed his eyes.

"He didn't get any of the chicks, did he?" Tristan asked breathlessly.

"I don't think so—I didn't count them, but the hen seems to have settled. She must have accounted for them all."

He didn't get a one, Thomas answered, fanning his whiskers in satisfaction. *Stupid dwarf dog.*

"Under the coop itself?" Blais mused. "Why didn't we see the burrow?"

You didn't see the one under the back of the cottage either, Thomas said, washing a paw.

"Under the *cottage?*" Tristan asked, shocked.

You wouldn't look there, Thomas said offhandedly. *You only checked to see whether he'd been near the chickens. He was right under your nose all the time. Which, considering your nose, was easy enough. Plenty of room there.*

Half a minute of following his long nose around the edge of the cottage led Tristan to the fox's burrow. The entrance was behind the rain barrel and very well hidden.

"I'll get dirt and rocks to stop it up," Tristan said.

Blais snorted. "I think I can manage one more spell today." He used a handful of dirt and pebbles. The hole vanished entirely as Blais spoke the spell. "Every time we set wards, the fox was already *inside* them, so they were useless," the wizard said. "Clever beast. But how did you know where his den was?"

"Thomas told me."

Blais stared at him. It must look, Tristan thought, like another pathetic plea to let the cat stay. He met his master's gaze uncertainly. Finally, Tristan cleared his throat.

"I ought to take him back to Dunehollow now. Come on, Thomas."

"Tristan. Wait." Blais was looking from the cat to the sealed den. "How do you mean, he *told* you?"

"He…*told* me. Under my nose, he said." Tristan's mouth twisted. "I expect he thinks a *cow* could hide under my nose, but I let it pass. He *did* save the chicks, after all."

Thomas licked a paw, pretending not to know he was being discussed.

"You didn't just see him go to the den, or something like that?" Blais persisted.

"No." What was Blais getting at? "He just told me it was under the cottage. Master, what's the matter?"

"You don't mean he *speaks?*" Blais' expression was odder by the moment.

"Well, not out loud." Tristan had never given the issue much thought. "It's more in my head."

"How *long* has he been talking in your head?" Blais' expression was intent.

"Always," Tristan answered honestly. He'd never thought it was the least bit odd. "Since the first time we met, I mean." A wizard was expected to be precise. Apprentices needed to practice that. He tipped his head to one side. "You mean *you* don't hear him?"

Blais sat down. He began to rub his nose once more. "Wizards can be blind. And all too plainly, deaf as well."

Tristan went to Thomas and picked the cat up. Thomas began to purr against his chest. "It's a longish walk to the village. I'll be back in time to cook supper, sir. I promise I won't dawdle."

Blais wasn't done with him. "When you said the cat promised you he wouldn't hunt birds—that was true, wasn't it? Thomas truly *did* give you his word?"

Tristan nodded uncertainly. Thomas purred like an immense bee in his arms.

"And we can trust that word, though I expect Minstrel will try him sorely. They'll torment one another, if I judge that bird rightly." Blais shook his head. "Tristan, have you read what a familiar is?"

"An animal at the command of a wizard," Tristan recited. "Well, not just *any* animal. Familiars are smart animals, or powerful ones. Familiars link wizards to earth magics, animal magics."

How demeaning. Thomas nibbled experimentally on Tristan's sleeve.

"All that and more," Blais told him. "Familiars can be of great use and value to a wizard. The sort of familiar a wizard can summon is determined by his powers, his skill. But a familiar that choose the *wizard* is always the most valuable of all."

"Chooses *me?*" Tristan could not take it in. He felt a warmth in his chest, just under the cat. It wasn't, he thought, only fur.

"I suspect so. Thomas speaks to *you.* He serves *you.* You say he protected you, in the bogland." Blais frowned. "I certainly cannot send a familiar away from his chosen wizard."

Tristan felt his mouth fall open.

"So, I suppose I'll have to take his word about not hunting birds," Blais said. "Just so long as Thomas isn't offended by a Protection spell or two on Minstrel's cage."

I'm sure I won't be, Thomas said, his eyes blissful green slits. Tristan started to shush him—then remembered that Blais couldn't hear the cat. But *he* could. He certainly could. Which was only proper. After all, Thomas was his very own familiar.

THE FULL MOON

The full moon played hide and seek with the clouds. When it shone clear, the beach was white and smooth as a bedsheet. Tracks stitched across it, as Tristan made a slow search for sea-smoothed pebbles. A full moon did not always bring the same magics an eclipse would, but there were always useful things to be gathered from a moonlit beach.

Tristan looked wistfully at the moon. It was bright enough to make his eyes water. He couldn't look long enough to see shapes in it. That swelling curve might be the unicorn's neck, or its arched back. It might be the banner of its silken tail.

His nights in the bog, his whole hasty quest, seemed more like a dream to Tristan with every hour that passed. Each night the moon grew larger. Each night his memories dimmed a little more. Had it not been for Thomas' witness to the events, Tristan would have doubted that he'd ever left the cottage while Blais was away. It wasn't as if he had anything to show for the adventure.

Tristan shook his head at himself and went on seeking magic pebbles. These, that looked so pink even in the moonlight were especially choice. Blais used them to craft love charms. The maidens of Dunehollow paid dear for those—all the men of Dunehollow followed the sea, one way and another. Sailors were known to be fickle as the sea they sailed upon. The more pink pebbles Tristan could find, the better off he and Blais would be.

Thomas had been stalking crabs. Now he was playing with something shiny. A fish, stranded by a wave? Tristan strolled over, curious. If it was a *big* fish, maybe Thomas would share.

The cat backed away, giving him an odd look.

The object wasn't a fish. Tristan knelt for a better look. It was metal, whatever it was. *Silver.* Even before he touched it, Tristan knew that.

It looked like a buckle. It was large enough to cover the palm of his hand. Its shape was sleek and flowing, its design a unicorn curved into an endless circle. The tip of the horn touched the last hairs of the silver tail.

Tristan looked up at the silver moon. He still couldn't see any sort of shape in it—but he knew the moonshine was back where it belonged.

The buckle was by way of a gift. The waves had cast it up to order, for him to find. Their mistress overhead, who ruled the tides of the sea, had so instructed them. The gift was a keepsake of an adventure, the remembrance of a friend.

The silver was warm under Tristan's fingers. It shone like the moon. Exactly like the moon.

AUTHOR'S NOTE

Moonshine came to be because a well-known children's publisher told my agent they'd consider a mid-grade book, preferably with a unicorn in it. They had liked *Thistledown* rather well, but felt it was "too old" for their readers.

I won't pretend I studied up on just what a mid-grade book was, or set out to write one. I chose to tell an early adventure of Tristan's, of the time when he and Thomas first met. And the well-known publisher decided the time wasn't right to add a hardcover fantasy to their line. So *Moonlight* became an early Print On Demand book from Wildside Press in 2001.

I hope you will agree that it's a tale readers of all ages will enjoy!

Visit my website CalandraEsdragon.weebly.com